Out of the corner of his eyes Biggles saw Dick go over-board and disappear under the foam, but he could do nothing to help him. Indeed, as he fought to keep the flying-boat under control, it seemed certain that during the next minute or two the others must join him. Ashen, he looked at Algy. 'Jump when she hits!' he cried, in a shrill, strangled voice, and dived deliberately at the rocks.

He did not quite reach them. The machine struck the sea a few yards short, but the result of the impact was almost the same as if she'd struck solid earth. There was a rending crash as the wings tore off at the roots, and the bows crumpled like a crushed eggshell.

Captain W. E. Johns was born in Hertfordshire in 1893. He flew with the Royal Flying Corps in the First World War and made a daring escape from a German prison camp in 1918. Between the wars he edited *Flying* and *Popular Flying* and became a writer for the Ministry of Defence. The first Biggles story, *Biggles the Camels are Coming* was published in 1932, and W. E. Johns went on to write a staggering 102 Biggles titles before his death in 1968.

www.kidsatrandomhouse.co.uk

BIGGLES BOOKS
PUBLISHED IN THIS EDITION

BIGGLES
flies WEST

CAPTAIN W.E. JOHNS

RED FOX

Red Fox would like to express their grateful thanks
for help given in the preparation of these editions to Jennifer Schofield,
author of *By Jove, Biggles*, Linda Shaughnessy of A. P. Watt Ltd
and especially to the late John Trendler.

BIGGLES FLIES WEST
A RED FOX BOOK 1 86 230222 7

First published in Great Britain by Oxford University Press, 1937

This Red Fox edition published 2004

Red Fox Books are published by Random House Children's Books,
61–63 Uxbridge Road, London W5 5SA,
a division of The Random House Group Ltd,
in Australia by Random House Australia (Pty) Ltd,
20 Alfred Street, Milsons Point, Sydney, NSW 2061, Australia,
in New Zealand by Random House New Zealand Ltd,
18 Poland Road, Glenfield, Auckland 10, New Zealand,
and in South Africa by Random House (Pty) Ltd,
Endulini, 5A Jubilee Road, Parktown 2193, South Africa

THE RANDOM HOUSE GROUP Limited Reg. No. 954009

A CIP catalogue record for this book is available from the British Library.

Printed and bound in Great Britain by
Cox and Wyman Ltd, Reading, Berkshire,

Contents

The moon is up, the stars are bright,
  The wind is fresh and free;
We're out to seek for gold to-night
  Across the silver sea.
The world was growing grey and old;
  Break out the sails again!
We're out to seek a realm of gold
  Beyond the Spanish Main.

ALFRED NOYES: *Drake*

Prologue

I. *Murder on the Main*

There was a soft creaking of blocks and tackle as the two ships, *Rose of Bristol* and *Santa Anna*, stirred uneasily on the gently heaving ocean. The ropes of the grappling irons that held them in a fast embrace grew taut, slackened, and grew taut again; it was almost as if the *Rose* shrank from the contact and strove to escape. But the steel hooks in her gunwales held her fast.

Overhead, from horizon to horizon, the sky was the deep azure blue of the tropics, unbroken except in the distant west, where, high above the misty peaks of Hispaniola,* a fleecy cloud was sailing slowly eastward. Nearer, a snow-white albatross swung low on rigid wings, its shadow sweeping the limpid surface of the sea, clear aquamarine, with little purple shadows here and there between the ripples that lapped gently at the *Santa*'s stern, or broke when a school of dolphins hurried by.

This scene of grace and colour was well matched by the splendour of the Spanish ship, a stately galleon, her counter red and silver, her towering poop all gold-encrusted, her sails, now loosely furled, rich cream and crimson, bright pennants streaming from her mastheads to the coats of arms that lined her sides above the bristling guns.

Only the *Rose*, belying her name, looked out of place, as out of place as a tramp on the threshold of a palace. Her sea-stained canvas, torn and shot-holed, lay in piles about the

---

* Now Haiti.

foot of her broken and splintered mainmast, or trailed with twisted skeins of cordage over her sides. From her bluff, Bristol-built bows to her sweeping stern she was painted black, a fitting colour, for about her well-scrubbed decks, in a welter of fast congealing blood, lay her crew, their glazing eyes upturned to the grim emblem of piracy that hung limply from the galleon's peak – a sable flag with a white device: the dreaded skull and crossbones.

The scene was all too common in the days when Charles the Second was king. The *Rose of Bristol*, a barque of two hundred and fifty tons, homeward bound from the Spanish Main, had fallen in with the *Santa Anna*, lately captured by the most notorious pirate on the coast: Louis Dakeyne, leader of the Brethren, half French, half Dutch, half man, half devil, whose name was execrated wherever sailors met between the Old World and the New; for he spared neither man nor maid, or old or young of any nationality. His latest exploit, so it was rumoured, had been the capture, off Cartagena, of the galleon *Santa Anna*, to which, after subjecting her captain to unspeakable tortures, he had transferred his cut-throat crew. So when at dawn the foretop of the Spaniard had appeared above the clear horizon, John Chandler, Master of the *Rose*, had clapped on sail and fled, knowing that, outmanned and outgunned, he stood no chance against the monster with its heavy metal and swarming crowd of villains. And for a time it seemed as if he would escape, for the barque was the better sailer of the two; but then the breeze that could have saved him passed him by, and while he had lain becalmed the bigger vessel with its enormous spread of canvas had crept slowly nearer, and with sinking heart the English captain knew his hour had come. With steady voice he had called his crew to prayer, then bade them die like men.

He had fought to the end, refusing to strike his colours,

8

firing his one small piece of ordnance until the pirates poured aboard. Then, with his loyal crew around him, he had made his last stand near the mainmast, neither asking nor giving quarter. Cutlass in hand, the name of his God on his lips, he had done all that one man could do while his gallant hands were beaten down and slain, and only he remained, to fall at length under a foul blow from behind.

But not to die at once. Sorely wounded, he was dragged aboard the galleon while his ship was looted. This done, he was questioned by Dakeyne about other ships in harbour, soon to sail for England; but he set his lips in an obstinate line and not a word came from them. At that they flogged him until he swooned, but they could not make him speak. And now, the pirate's patience soon exhausted, he stood upon the fatal plank, looking death in the face, with his hands tied behind his back.

A sudden silence fell, a hush broken only by the plaintive cry of the seabird, now circling very near, and the gentle murmur of the water far below.

Well might it have been for Louis Dakeyne, Louis le Grande, self-styled, or Louis the Exterminator, as many called him, had he dispatched his prisoner there and then, for the English mariner had still one card to play, and he played it with such deadly calm that those who heard his words turned pale, knowing that one on the point of death must speak the truth.

Turning from the end of the plank that hung far over the limpid sea so that he faced his ship, he regarded the grinning mob, his captors, with steadfast eyes that held not fear, nor hate, but scorn and triumph. For a moment he stood thus while a bead of blood crept down his ashen brow, crossing a cut so that a cross of red was formed.

The omen did not pass unseen, and a low mutter, like breakers on a distant beach, ran through the mob. It died away to silence as the stricken captain spoke.

'Harken unto me, black hounds of hell,' he cried, in a clear, ringing voice. 'Harken at these my words, for they will be in the ears of each and all of you when your hour comes, as it will, before another moon shall wax and wane.'

A howl of derision rose into the sun-soaked air.

'Shoot him,' screamed one.

'*Perro! Vamos a ver,**' snarled a renegade Spaniard.

'Swing him by the heels,' roared a one-eyed monster.

'Woodle him,**' bawled another.

'Silence!' At the pirate captain's sharp command the imprecations ceased. He was watching the doomed man with a peculiar expression, not far removed from fear, upon his face.

'Amongst the gold that you have taken from my ship and put with yours,' went on the English captain dispassionately, 'there is one coin, a gold doubloon, that carries all your fates, for it is cursed. When Joseph Bawn, a red-haired thief whom some of you may know, was brought to the scaffold at Port Royal this day last week, that coin was in his pocket. And there, within the shadow of the gallows, he spat upon it thrice. And as he spat he cursed the God who made him, and everyone into whose hands the gold should fall.'

A shudder, like the sound of the wind in leafless trees, ran through the superstitious audience.

'That piece was put upon my ship because it was the

---

* Spanish: 'Dog! We'll see about that.'
** 'Woodling' was a barbarous form of torture favoured by buccaneers to induce prisoners to divulge the hiding places of their valuables. (Naturally, in the sacking of a ship, or town, those who possessed gold or jewels hid them in the hope that they would not be found.) Woodling, the process employed to make them speak, consisted of tying a piece of cord round the prisoner's brows, and then screwing it up with a piece of wood, like a tourniquet. WEJ

king's and had to go to England,' continued the captain relentlessly. 'Mark well my fate, and see how true the curse is working; then contemplate your own that soon must follow. For you can not escape. The piece is in your hoard, and to disown it you must throw your treasure overboard, which you have not the heart to do.'

There was no more laughing. Upon the faces of the pirates were frowns and scowls; upon their lips were oaths, but in their hearts cold fear.

John Chandler lifted his blue eyes to the blue sky. 'With my last breath I beseech my God to strengthen now that curse until—'

He got no farther. Dakeyne's pistol blazed. A stream of flame and sparks leapt from its gaping muzzle and ended at the sailor's breast.

For an instant he remained standing, eyes upturned, lips moving. Then his knees bent; his body sagged limply and plunged down into the void.

At the sound of the splash the pirates rushed to the side of their ship, eyes seeking the corpse. But all they saw was an ever-spreading ring of ripples that circled slowly outwards from a crimson stain. And as they stared aghast an icy slant of wind moaned through the rigging.

'What's that?' muttered Dakeyne, white-faced.

'The bird! It was the albatross!' cried Jamaica Joe, his quartermaster.

The pirate's eyes flashed round the sky. 'The bird has gone!' he gasped. 'Look!'

There was a sudden hush as all eyes followed his quivering forefinger.

Far to the west, from north to south, across the sky, an indigo belt was racing low towards them, blotting out the blue.

The pirate's voice scarce rose above the hubbub. 'All

hands aloft,' he croaked through lips that were suddenly dry.

II. *The Curse*

In setting down the disasters that befell the *Santa Anna* following immediately after the murder of Captain John Chandler, it is not suggested that these were caused directly by the sacrilegious words of a drunken buccaneer on the scaffold at Port Royal, but that they were the indirect cause is certain.

There is no question about the incident happening. We know from the famous chronicles of Exquemelin, the surgeon who served under the most notorious pirate captains, including the celebrated Morgan, and who afterwards wrote an account of his adventures, that Joseph Bawn was a pirate of the most villainous type. We know that he was turned off* at Port Royal in January 1689, for the foul murder of a comrade whose rations he had tried to steal, and Sir John Modyford, Governor of Jamaica at that time, refers to the condemned pirate's frightful curse in a letter to Lord Arlington, Secretary of State to Charles II's 'Cabal' Cabinet. But to presume that the last wish of a red-handed murderer was fulfilled by his Maker would be going too far. As far as the *Santa Anna* was concerned, the truth is probably to be found in four perfectly natural causes.

In the first place there was the incident itself, which distracted the attention of every soul on board, including the watch, so that the hurricane caught them unprepared. Secondly, there was the ship. Like all Spanish ships of the period she was unseaworthy; the high poop and short keel were so opposed to all natural laws that one marvels that

---

* ie hanged.

they sailed at all. Thirdly, the firmly ingrained superstitions of the crew – notwithstanding their professed godlessness – must be taken into account. And lastly, but by no means least, their lack of discipline or control.

From the years 1680 to 1720, when piracy was in its heyday, it would be no exaggeration to say that the Brethren of the Coast – as they called themselves – were virtually in command of the West Indies and the Spanish Mainland. Morgan was probably more powerful in Jamaica than the Governor; he certainly had more men at his beck and call. That he was superior to the Spanish colonists is proved by his exploits, which included the taking and sacking of such cities as Panama, Porto Bello, and Maracaibo; Panama was the most strongly fortified city on the Main. At Tortuga, the Brethren had practically established a colony of their own, and that they did not, in fact, do so, was due to the weakness already referred to – lack of discipline.

Their commanders were appointed by themselves and held their posts only by the goodwill of the crews. Such orders as they gave, except in the heat of battle, were, in fact, only suggestions, for if they did not meet with the approval of the ship's companies they were not carried out. If the captain dared to insist, more often than not he was deposed, sometimes by the simple expedient of being thrown overboard. Admittedly, in times of success, orders were, on the whole, obeyed, but when things started going wrong the officers had to look to the priming of their pistols. It is on record that one pirate ship had no less than thirteen captains in a few months. Bartholomew Roberts, who maintained his command for four years, probably held the record for duration of office – popular fiction notwithstanding.

At the time of the capture of the *Rose of Bristol* the popularity of Louis Dakeyne ran high, for a very good reason. The *Santa Anna*, which he had waylaid, had proved to be a veritable treasure ship, laden with such minted coins as doubloons, golden moidores, pieces of eight, and cross money, to say nothing of plate, silks, lace, and other rare fabrics that would fetch good money at Port Royal, where unscrupulous traders were making fortunes. In their minds, Dakeyne's *matelots** – as the pirates sometimes called themselves – were already spending their ill-gotten gains in the iniquitous and pestilential drinking booths that lined the waterfront, so it may be safely assumed that the bare possibility of this depraved ambition being frustrated soon set them grumbling.

When the hurricane struck the galleon she heeled over until the grapnels tore the side clean out of the English ship. The foresail, carelessly stowed, burst like a paper bag, flinging overboard two men, who soon disappeared astern in the smother of foam whipped up from the surface of the sea. By an odd coincidence they were two of the very men who had clamoured for the English captain's instant death as he stood on the plank, a fact that was not overlooked by the rest of the crew, who saw in the disaster the direct hand of God. Meanwhile the *Santa Anna* heeled away before a wind of such violence as no man on board had ever before experienced. It beat up terrific seas that poured over the poop and splashed half way up the mainmast.

For seven days the tempest raged, and in that time nine men were killed. The rest were so exhausted that they could hardly stand, much less keep the ship clear of water.

On the fifth day a deputation, headed by the quartermaster, had staggered to the captain, imploring him to throw all the gold overboard that their lives might be spared. Dakeyne refused peremptorily to jettison what had cost so much blood and toil to get. The men grumbled, the

* French: sailors.

quartermaster louder than the rest, and Dakeyne, seeing in him as the only other navigator a likely rival, had pistolled him on the spot.

On the eighth day the wind died away, and the galleon lay becalmed on a sea that was as flat as a sheet of glass. She was short of water and short of provisions. What little water she had left was foul, and the food, badly cured *boucan*,* was rotten and full of maggots, due to the damp heat. The muttering grew ominous.

By nightfall the crew had split into two parties, those who wished to jettison the treasure and those who sided with the captain. The latter were in the minority. Fighting broke out more than once, and several men were killed. Their bodies, after the custom of the pirates, were flung overboard. And all the time the ship lay like a log on the glassy sea while sharks gathered round to enjoy a grisly feast.

When the calm had lasted for six days Dakeyne lived up to the reputation that had earned for him his sinister nickname of Exterminator. While the larger party were together in the fo'castle, plotting, no doubt, Dakeyne and his adherents crept upon them with loaded muskets and delivered such a volley that half of them fell dead or dying. The rest were easily dispatched. More bodies were flung overboard, and the number of sharks increased. Eleven men only remained alive, not counting the captain. Having no water, they drank rum, and, rolling drunk, consoled themselves by roaring Morgan's famous slogan, coined after the dreadful sacking of Porto Bello:

> If there be few amongst us
> Our hearts are very great;
> And each will have more plunder,
> And each will have more plate.

* Salted beef.

Their hearts were not very great on the morrow. Louis the Exterminator whistled for a wind. He whistled in vain.

A blood-red sun was sinking into a blood-red sea the following evening when the pirate captain, a scarlet bandanna tied about his head, called to one of the men who were lounging listlessly aft to bring him a drink of rum. His throat, he declared, was parched – as well it might be after the quantity of liquor he had already drunk that day. The man fetched the rum bottle and passed it to the captain. But he did not watch him drink it. His eyes were on the back of the captain's hand as it rested on the rail, and had Dakeyne been sober he might have remarked the seaman's expression. But he did not. It is doubtful even if he had noticed what the sailor had seen – a round patch of what looked like white dust on the back of his hand.

The sailor, a Frenchman who had sailed with L'Ollonois, returned swiftly to the others. With ashen face and staring eyes he told them what he had seen. 'It is the plague,' he muttered hoarsely.

Lorton, a one-armed gunner who had sailed many seas, sprang to his feet, an oath on his lips, hand groping for his knife; but the Frenchman restrained him, casting furtive glances over his shoulder in case the captain should be watching.

That night, while Dakeyne was heavy in drunken sleep, the remnant of the crew launched the one boat that had escaped damage by the storm, and stole away across a moonlit sea, not knowing that the sun had warped the planks and opened up the seams. For three days of purgatory they kept the boat afloat by constant bailing before they were picked up by a Spanish ship, whose commander, being a humane man, hanged them out of hand instead of subjecting them to the usual tortures.

Dakeyne awoke to find himself alone and all the rum

gone. All that day he moped about; but during the night came another storm, as furious as the last. For a time he tried to work the ship alone, but at length his strength gave out and he staggered to his cabin to rest.

When he awoke he was surprised to find that the rolling had ceased, and going up on deck, saw that a remarkable thing had happened, so remarkable that he could scarcely believe his good fortune. The ship was aground on an island the size of which he could not judge; more than that, she was high and dry where the tide had left her. What was still more surprising, she appeared to be in a land-locked harbour, an inlet so small that at first he could not understand how she had got there. Presently, exploring, the apparent miracle was explained.

The galleon had drifted into a narrow channel between grey rocks about the same height as herself, which opened out at the inner end into a sort of miniature lagoon. He could not see the sea, but he could hear it, a short distance away. The rocks on either side were so close that he could jump ashore, which presently he did, to make certain that no Indians were hidden in the jungle that crowded nearly to the water's edge. From a comfortable seat on a rock he regarded the ship and her position with considerable satisfaction. Never were Morgan's words more appropriate, he reflected, for now there was only one to share the treasure, and it was he. If the ship had come in it could be got out, he opined, not unreasonably. There was bound to be food and water on the island. He would fill the casks and lay in a store of provisions, and then sail the ship to a proper harbour. By thunder, so he would! He'd show them what one man could do. Dakeyne was no coward or he would not have been the captain of a pirate crew.

It would not take him long to work out his position, he thought, and he was about to put this plan into execution when he remembered something that caused a cold shiver to run down his spine. Bawn's doubloon! The curse, the potency of which he could no longer ignore. It would be the act of a madman to set off on such a voyage as the one he proposed with that dreadful piece of gold on board. No matter. There was an easy way of getting over that difficulty. He would put the doubloons ashore, every jack one of 'em; hide 'em until such time as he could come back with a stout ship and a stout-hearted crew to retrieve them.

He set to work with commendable method and determination, but he had neither the time nor inclination to dig a hole; instead, he selected a depression in the rocks, a hole large enough to take perhaps two or three casks lying one on top of another, and into this he began to pour the coins. He did not like the idea of handling the gold, and he looked at the minted pieces suspiciously as he scooped them into the piece of canvas he was using as a carrier; but his heart grew lighter with each load he carried, hoping that the treacherous piece was already in the hole.

It took him a long time to transfer them all, for the gold was heavy and the sun was hot; but at last the job was done. Then, too wise to trust his memory, he sat down at the Spanish captain's desk and began to make a note of the exact position of the hole in which the treasure lay, the note taking the form of a rough map to which bearings and measurements could afterwards be added.

While thus engaged it struck him suddenly that all was strangely quiet, unnaturally quiet; also, for no apparent reason, the temperature had dropped several degrees, causing the sweat on his face to turn cold and clammy. It sent a shiver running through him, leaving as an aftermath an apprehension of danger. But as we have already observed, Louis the Exterminator was no coward. His jaw set at an ugly angle as he primed and cocked his pistol; then, with a faint sneer curling the corners of his loose mouth, he crept quietly up the companion and looked around.

Not a soul was in sight. Not a movement could he see. Not a sound could he hear but the sullen murmur of the sea against the rocks outside the little inlet. Satisfied that all was well, he returned to the cabin, but before he could resume his task a sudden cry outside brought him round with a nervous start. Pistol in hand, he strode swiftly to one of the poop lights.

His face paled as a snow-white albatross sailed slowly past his field of vision. There seemed to be something familiar about it. Was it imagination or was it the same bird that had hovered round the ill-fated *Rose of Bristol*? He could not be sure, but a superstitious conscience tugged his heart-strings and the presentiment of an unseen danger still persisted. For a moment or two he waited, pistol at the ready, hoping that the bird would come within range. Whether the ball struck it or not, he would derive some satisfaction from having alarmed it, he thought savagely. But no such opportunity presented itself. It was almost as if the great bird understood what was passing in his mind, for it banked slowly to and fro just out of range, turning its head all the while to watch him in a curiously human manner, from time to time uttering its mournful cry.

The Exterminator spat contemptuously, but he could not deceive himself. For the first time in his life he was afraid, afraid of he knew not what. He hurried back to the desk, propped the pistol against a heavy church candlestick that stood within easy reach, and picked up the quill to finish marking out his map. As he did so, something dropped heavily out of the gathered-in part of his silken doublet. Idly, he looked to see what it was. But as his eyes came to rest on the object he caught his breath sharply; the pupils of his eyes dilated and his face set in lines of unspeakable horror. The object was a gold doubloon.

For a few moments he continued to stare at it unbelievingly. Then, with an oath, he sprang to his feet. His eyes did not leave the coin. It seemed to fascinate him. He knew what it was. He did not know how he knew, but he *knew*. Knew that the one coin that had slipped out of the canvas carrier was THE coin. The doubloon to which still clung the dying pirate's curse. Somehow it had dropped into one of the many pleats of his doublet. To what purpose?

Had he been less enthralled by the crudely cut piece of gold he might have seen. He might have noticed that his trembling hand was resting on the desk, and the slight vibration was causing the muzzle of the pistol to slip. At first it moved very slowly, hesitatingly, but as it passed the point of balance it dropped sharply, with a thud. The weapon roared. A tongue of blood-red flame spurted from the gaping muzzle. For a fleeting instant it seemed to lick the pirate's silken doublet Then it was gone. Silence fell. A sickly smell of scorching mingled with the acrid reek of powder-smoke.

For perhaps three seconds after his first convulsive spasm of agony the pirate did not move. Then, his staring eyes still fixed on the coin, his right hand crept down until it rested on the dreadful hole made by the pistol ball. Slowly, as if he feared what he might see, he looked down, and saw his life-blood pumping through his grimy fingers. At the sight, the horror on his ashen face gave way to hopeless resignation. He sank down in the chair and covered his face with his hands. No sound broke the silence except a sinister drip – drip – drip. A little crimson pool began to form at his feet.

Slowly, so slowly that the movement was hardly perceptible, his body began to sag forward until at length it lay asprawl the desk. A fly settled on the pallid, red-streaked face, but the pirate did not move. Others joined it. Still he did not move.

There was a flash of white as the albatross swept past the open port. Louis le Grande did not see it; nor did he hear the cry that seemed to swell to a note of triumph as it soared into the sun-drenched blue of heaven.

Inside the cabin settled the hush that comes with the presence of Death. A hush that was to remain unbroken for just two hundred and fifty years.

III. *Time Marches On*

The years rolled by, and with their passing, nature triumphed. Came sun and rain and wind and calm, but no man came to the island where Louis, once le Grande, kept lonely vigil with his fate.

Before a year was out the gruesome stains upon the galleon's deck were hidden beneath a mantle of fallen leaves that died and rotted where they lay, and made a sure foundation for the ever-questing moss.

When James the Second ruled in England there came a storm that undermined the rocks which lay about the harbour's narrow mouth, so that they fell, and falling, made a wall against the waves; and year by year the tireless sea cemented them with sand.

The years rolled on, each year contributing its little to the shrouding of the dying ship. While Queen Anne wore the crown came briers and vines to seek a foothold in the moss that blanketed the rotting timbers. In the reign of George the First the masts collapsed and struck a futile blow at the all-devouring jungle; but the briers and vines and weeds embraced them, and dragged them down to oblivion and decay.

The years rolled on. In the reign of George the Second a ship came watering at the island, and although the thirsty sailors came ashore they did not learn its secret. When George the Third was king came several ships, but a hundred years had passed and no sign remained to reveal what they could not suspect, and so they sailed away.

The years rolled on. When George the Fourth sat on the throne a shipwrecked mariner was cast away upon the island, and although he stayed there for a year, often in his lonely wanderings passing within a score of paces of the green-girt wreck, he did not find it. And so he went away in the next ship that called, and in due course died a pauper's death, not knowing that once he had made a frugal meal within a yard of enough doubloons to pay a prince's ransom.

The years rolled on. William the Fourth, Victoria, King Edward – the seventh of the name – King George the Fifth, the eighth King Edward, all ruled in turn, but still the island kept its secret.

And then one day, when George the Sixth upheld the British Empire, a man came running on the rocks, a sailor, judging by his clothes. And as he ran he gasped for breath, and looked behind as one who runs in fear. Reaching the rock on which Dakeyne once stood, he turned towards the briers and vines as if to seek a hiding place. A little dell of green moss beckoned, and bracing himself, he jumped. He landed fair and square, but stumbled as the rotting timbers which the moss concealed collapsed beneath his weight. A scream of mortal fear broke from his lips as he clutched at the air for support. But the effort was in vain, and he plunged headlong into the void.

Thus was the silence broken.

Chapter 1

An Ugly Customer

Through the fog-frosted glass of his attic window Dick Denver stared with unseeing eyes at the muddy water of the River Thames as it surged sullenly through the grey November murk towards the sea. Only fifteen years of life lay behind him; how many lay ahead he did not know, nor did he care, and the despondency of his mood was reflected in his thin, pale face.

In the years that were gone he had known at least a few happy hours, the all-too-brief spells when his sailor father had come home from the deep seas, but now there would be no more. A horror that had haunted him ever since he was old enough to know that ships were sometimes wrecked had come to pass. The *Seadream* had made her last voyage and his father would come home no more. There would be no more counting the days until his return; no more scanning the shipping columns of the papers he sold for a living, seeking the name of his father's ship, and its position; no more watching for the *Seadream*'s blunt, rust-encrusted bows to come ploughing up the river; no more cheering at the wharf; no more long, after-supper talks about strange, foreign parts of the world. No more. Those days had gone, gone for good, and with them had gone the only thing that had made his life worth living – his father.

His mother he had never known. A hard-faced, bad-tempered woman had looked after him during his father's long absences at sea until he was thirteen; then she, too, had died, and thereafter he had fended for himself, maintaining a tiny attic in Wapping, overlooking the river, which his father shared when he was home.

But the struggle for existence had been a hard one, and although his short fair hair was neatly brushed, and his clear blue eyes alert, his cheeks were pale and pinched from under-nourishment. His clothes were, as might be expected, threadbare, and did little either to protect his body, or improve his down-and-out appearance. Dick was, in fact, down – down in the depths of despondency; but he was far from out.

He had first read of the wreck of the *Seadream* in one of the papers he had been selling, and the memory of that dreadful moment still kept him awake at night. Then, weeks afterwards, had come the joyful news that his father had been one of the two or three survivors and was in hospital at Boston, in America. This had been followed by more weeks of silence and suspense that had only an hour before been ended by the arrival at his dingy room of an unknown sailor who had broken the terrible news that his father, exhausted by privations as a castaway after the wreck, had died. At least, that was the official story, but the sailor, whose name Dick had forgotten to ask, had told a different tale.

That it was true Dick had no reason to doubt, for the sailor had brought him a letter from his father, which now lay on the deal table in front of him. He had – so the sailor had said – handed it to him on his deathbed, charging him to give it to his son when he returned to London. These instructions the sailor had obeyed faithfully, as a service from one sailor to another, and thereafter departed, Dick knew not whither.

The circumstances of his father's death were as painful as they were mysterious, for he had died, not in hospital as might have been supposed, but in a low dive on the waterfront. The sailor had told him how he also had spent the night in the dive while looking for a ship, but in the early hours of the morning he had been awakened by low moans coming from the next room. Upon investigation he had found a British sailor named Jack Denver, Dick's father, bleeding to death from a knife thrust in the back; but before he had died he had handed him the letter, asking him as a favour to deliver it into the hands of his son, at Number I, Bride's Alley, Wapping, on his return to the Port of London. The sailor, who had left Boston on the next tide, true to his word, had delivered the letter, which still lay unopened on the table.

Why he had not opened it Dick did not know. Possibly it was because he felt that once the letter was opened, it would be the end. While it remained sealed there would still be a final message to look forward to from the only human being he had ever loved. So he had hesitated, trying to prolong the pleasure that was really agony.

For the hundredth time he picked up the envelope, turning it over and over in his hands. It was bulky, and heavy, with the name and address written faintly in lead pencil. He recognized his father's handwriting, but he knew that he must have been very weak when he had written it, for normally his writing was bold and decisive.

The hoarse hoot of a ship's siren made him glance through the window again, and he saw the bulk of a deep-sea tramp steamer, huge and distorted in the gloom, creeping out on the tide. The picture would have been a dismal one at any time, but now it was depressing in the extreme. The mist, which was really a fine drizzle, hung low, like dirty yellow smoke, saturating everything with its clammy moisture. The water dripped slowly from the eaves, splashed monotonously from the leaky spouting and ran in tiny rivulets down the window panes. Far away on the other side of the river a line of dim, yellow sparks showed where the street lamps were being lighted.

From the contemplation of this miserable scene Dick was suddenly interrupted by a sound that brought a perplexed frown to his forehead, for it was a noise that he seldom heard. Heavy footsteps were coming up the stairs; loud, clumsy footsteps, as if the feet were unaccustomed to thick boots or narrow stairs. That they were coming to his room was certain, for the staircase was a cul-de-sac that ended in the attic. Who could it be? His heart gave a lurch and his hands began to tremble, as the deliberate tread on the bare boards struck a chord in his memory. It reminded him of his father.

Dropping the letter among some unsold papers that lay scattered on the far side of the table, he walked quickly to the door and threw it open just as a stranger arrived at the head of the stairs, and there was something so sinister in his manner and appearance that, prompted by an acute instinct of self-preservation, Dick recoiled backward into the room. The man followed until his bulk filled the narrow doorway, from where he regarded Dick with cold, questioning eyes, that slanted upwards at the ends in a manner that suggested remote oriental ancestry.

In stature he was short, but broad, and obviously of great physical strength, an impression that was emphasized by arms that hung nearly down to his knees, like those of a gorilla. Indeed, he was not unlike a great ape, for the backs of his hands, now slowly opening and closing, were covered with downy red hair. His face, like his body, was short and broad, with a wide, thin-lipped mouth that was not improved by a large, semicircular scar, like a crescent moon, at one corner. His eyebrows, the same colour as the hair on his hands, were straight, shaggy, and hung far over his little restless eyes. A greasy blue jersey covered his powerful torso and suggested that he was a seafaring man.

For a moment or two they regarded each other speculatively, and then the stranger spoke.

'What's your name, pup?' he asked slowly, in a low, expressionless voice.

'Dick – Dick Denver,' replied Dick a trifle nervously, for although he was no coward there was something in the other's manner that alarmed him.

'Jack Denver's brat, eh?'

'Jack Denver was my father.'

'Him as was on the *Seadream*?'

'Yes – that's right.'

'Joe Dawkin 'as been 'ere to see you, ain't he?'

Dick shook his head. 'I've never heard of Joe Dawkin,' he answered truthfully.

'Well, you've had a sailor man 'ere?'

'Yes.'

'Brought you a letter from your old man?'

'Yes, he did.'

'Where is it?' The stranger fired out the words like pistol shots.

'Why, what's that got to do—'

'Never mind what that's got to do with me. Where is it?' The stranger seemed to force the words through his teeth, slowly, in a manner that was distinctly threatening.

'What do you want with it?'

'*Give it to me!*'

Dick's eyes flashed suddenly, and he set his teeth. 'No,' he said obstinately.

With horrible deliberation the other drew a heavy clasp knife from his pocket. A long, pointed blade jerked open with a click. 'So you won't, eh?' he said in the same monotonous undertone that he had first employed.

The wicked-looking blade seemed to fascinate Dick; he could not tear his eyes away from it. He was still staring at it when the sailor began to edge very slowly into the room, his

27

body bent forward, jaw out-thrust, his thin lips curled back in an animal snarl revealing two rows of broken, discoloured teeth.

For one dreadful moment Dick retreated before him, but when his groping hands touched the wall behind him and he knew he could go no farther he nearly fell into a panic. Picking up the one rickety chair the room possessed, he swung it with all his force against the window, and before the crash of falling glass had died away he had rushed to the spot. 'Help! Help!' he screamed.

He heard the sailor coming and leapt aside just in time. A whirling arm missed him by inches. But the sailor's quick rush had left the doorway open, and before he could prevent it Dick had ducked like lightning under the table and was streaking for the stairs like a rabbit going into its burrow. Nor did he stop when he reached them. Down he went, taking them four and five at a time at imminent risk of breaking his neck. Nor did he stop even when he reached the hall at the bottom. The front door stood wide open. Through it he dashed into the street, and turning sharply to the right, ran down the shining pavement in search of a policeman.

He had not gone a dozen yards, however, when his progress was cut short by a collision that knocked most of the breath out of him. Three figures emerged suddenly from the gloom as they walked briskly along the pavement; he tried to avoid them, but his feet slipped on the greasy stone, and almost before he knew what was happening he found himself being tightly held in a pair of strong arms.

'Hi, hi! Not so fast, my lad. What's all the hurry about?' said a quiet voice reproachfully, yet not without a twinge of humour.

Dick knew by the softly modulated tones that his captor was a gentleman, and he gave a gasp of relief. 'There's a man up in my room, sir,' he gasped desperately.

The other laughed softly. 'Well, I don't suppose he'll eat you,' he said cheerfully.

'He tried to kill me, though,' declared Dick bitterly.

'Tried to kill you?'

'Yes, sir.'

'How?'

'With a knife.'

'What made him try to do that?'

'He came to rob me.'

'Rob you?' There was incredulity in the question.

One of the others laughed. 'Of what?'

'A letter, sir. A letter I've just had from my father. Don't let him take it, sir,' pleaded Dick passionately.

'We'd better look into this, Algy,' muttered the man who held him, as he relaxed his grip. 'Where do you live, son?'

'Up here, sir, on the top floor.' Dick led the way to the sombre hall.

'Mind how you go, Biggles. It doesn't look too healthy in there to me,' said the youngest of the three strangers, who, Dick now saw, was not much older than himself.

'Fiddlesticks! We're in London, not Port Said,' was the curt reply. 'Come on.'

Dick followed his helpers to the top of the stairs. The landing was in darkness, but a narrow bar of light below the closed door suggested that someone was inside.

The one whom the others had called Biggles, a slim, clean-shaven man with a keen, thoughtful face, tried the door. It was locked. He struck a match and looked at Dick. 'Could he get away through a window?' he asked in a low voice.

'No, sir. It's a forty foot drop down to the street.'

'Good.' Biggles knocked sharply on a flimsy panel. 'Open this door,' he called loudly.

There was no reply.

'This is your room, you're sure of that?' Biggles asked Dick suspiciously.

'Yes, sir.'

'I mean – you rent it?'

'Yes, sir.'

'You're telling me the truth?'

'On my oath, sir.'

'All right! Stand back.' There was a splintering crash as Biggles hurled his weight against the door. It flew open and the scene within was revealed.

The stranger was standing by the table, with the letter, which presumably he had just found, in his left hand. The knife lay open on the table, and as his slanting eyes rested malevolently on the newcomers his right hand began to creep towards it.

'What are you doing in this lad's room?' asked Biggles sharply.

'That's no business of yourn,' growled the other, scowling.

'I'm sorry to disappoint you, my friend, but I happen to have made it my business,' rapped out Biggles coldly. 'Put that letter down.'

'I should say so.'

'There's no need for you to say so; I've already said it.'

'Are you looking fer trouble, Mr Nosey Parker?'

'If anyone is doing that, it's you. Come along, put the letter down and clear out. I don't want to make this a police court job any more than you do.'

An ugly sneer curled the sailor's lips. He picked up the knife. 'So that's your tune, is it?' he snarled.

'It's the only tune I've got for you.'

'Then let's see how you like this one,' grated the other, gripping the knife firmly and taking a pace forward.

Biggles did not move. 'Ginger, run down and fetch a policeman, will you?' he said quietly. 'And now, my man,' he resumed, as Ginger ran noisily down the wooden stairs, 'I'm going to give you a last chance. Put that letter on the table and the knife in your pocket, and you are free to go. Refuse, and I'll see to it that you are clapped somewhere where you won't be able to make a nuisance of yourself for a long time to come. We don't stand for robbery with violence in this country, as you'll soon learn to your cost. Now then, make up your mind. Which is it going to be?'

The sailor hesitated, looking from one to the other of the three figures framed in the doorway. Possibly he realized that even if he succeeded in passing them he might encounter a policeman before he reached the street. A moment later heavy footsteps on the stairs helped him to decide, for with a foul oath he flung the letter on the table and thrust the knife through his belt, under his jacket. 'I'll remember you the next time I see you, my cock,' he gritted vindictively. 'Maybe you won't chirp so loud then.'

'We'll talk about chirping when that time comes,' replied Biggles coolly.

'What's going on here?' demanded a fresh voice from the background. A policeman pushed his way to the front.

'It's all right, officer; I thought we were going to have a little trouble, but our seafaring friend here has thought better of it,' said Biggles quietly.

'Don't you want to charge him, sir?' There was genuine regret in the policeman's tone as he eyed the intruder with disfavour.

'No, he can go as far as I'm concerned.'

If looks could kill, Biggles would have been struck dead on the spot as the sailor passed between him and the constable and disappeared down the stairs.

Biggles put his hand in his pocket and slipped something into the policeman's palm. 'Sorry I had to trouble you,' he said softly. 'Much obliged for your assistance, but everything is all right now, I think.'

'Thank you, sir. Glad I could be of service,' replied the constable. 'If you don't mind, I'll slip along and keep an eye on that customer. I don't like the look of him,' he added quickly, as he followed the sailor down the stairs.

Biggles picked up the letter and handed it to Dick. 'Well, my lad, there's your letter,' he said. 'What was all the trouble about, anyway?'

'I don't know, sir, and that's a fact,' confessed Dick frankly.

'But why should a man risk putting his head into a noose in order to get what one can only suppose to be a purely personal message from your father to you?'

'That's more than I can say, sir,' replied Dick. 'You see, sir, my father is dead. A sailor brought the letter to me today; I haven't read it yet.'

'I see,' nodded Biggles. 'Well, maybe the thing will explain itself when you do read it. But we shall have to be getting along.' He turned towards the stairs when another thought seemed to strike him. 'What are you going to do, laddie?' he asked, looking back at Dick.

'I dunno, sir. I daren't stop here in case that sailor comes back and does me in.'

'Haven't you any friends or relatives where you can stay?'

'No, sir.'

'Any money?'

'No, sir.'

'None at all?'

'Only tuppence.'

'Humph! That won't see you very far, I'm afraid,' murmured Biggles.

'That's all right, sir. I'll doss down on the allotments,' declared Dick.

'*Where?*'

'In one of the gardening huts on the allotments. I'll go

32

round until I find one of 'em open. I've had to do it many a time before.'

Biggles made a grimace. 'Bless my heart and soul! I've slept rough myself on occasion, but this is no night for picnicking,' he declared. 'I tell you what. It must be about tea-time. Let's find a restaurant where we can talk things over while we have a bite of food. By the way, what's your name?'

'Dick, sir. Dick Denver.'

'Good! That's easy to remember,' smiled Biggles. 'We don't know our way very well in this part of the world, so perhaps you can guide us to a place where we can tear a plate of crumpets to pieces.'

Dick nodded, grinning broadly. 'I know 'em all, sir,' he declared promptly. 'There's Old Kate's at the corner. That's where I usually go because you can get sausage and mash there for fivepence a go. Bread a ha'penny extra. Or there's the "Jolly Shipmates" coffee tavern, but they charge a bob there and a penny for bread.'

Biggles smiled faintly. 'It sounds like the "Jolly Shipmates" to me,' he decided. 'I think we shall be able to raise a shilling apiece between us,' he added seriously. 'Come on.'

Chapter 2

The Doubloon

Dick led the way jubilantly, for it was not often that he was treated to a free meal, and in a few minutes they were all seated round a marble-topped table with their feet on a newly sawdusted floor. The place was fairly full, sailors and watermen forming the bulk of the customers, and the air was blue with tobacco smoke, but no-one paid any attention to them as they took their places in a quiet corner.

A pale-faced youth in a white apron waited on them.

'Sausage and mash for four, a pot of tea and plenty of bread,' ordered Biggles.

'While we are waiting, just to satisfy my curiosity, you might cast your eye over your father's letter,' suggested Algy to Dick. 'I've got an idea that that ugly-looking swab of a sailor had a reason for wanting to get hold of it – in fact, he must have had, and a very good one, too, or he wouldn't have gone to such lengths to get it.'

'All the same, my dad never had any money, so I don't see how it could be anything worth pinching,' replied Dick, taking the letter from his pocket. 'I dunno, though, it feels a bit heavy,' he went on quickly, with a sudden flash of interest. 'I believe there's something in it besides paper.'

As he spoke he slit the top of the envelope, rather carelessly. Instantly there was a yellow gleam as something fell out and rang musically on the marble top of the table.

In a flash Biggles's hand had shot out and covered it, just as the waiter hurried up with the four plates. Not until he had departed did Biggles lift his hand, disclosing what lay underneath. A low whistle left his lips. 'Oh-ho! Oh-ho!' he ejaculated quickly, and then cast a swift glance around. 'You'd better put that in your pocket, Dick,' he said in a low voice. 'This is no place to throw that sort of stuff about.'

'What sort of stuff?' asked Dick, agape, eyes on a roughly circular disk that lay on the table.

'Gold,' breathed Biggles.

Dick caught his breath. 'Gold!' he cried incredulously.

'Ssh, not so loud. There's no need to tell the world about it.'

'Go on, you're kidding,' muttered Dick unbelievingly.

Biggles shook his head. 'There's no kidding about that particular metal,' he murmured.

'But that isn't a sovereign, is it?' whispered Dick. 'I never saw one but once,' he added, by way of explanation.

'No, it isn't a sovereign,' agreed Biggles, 'but it's worth a good deal more. I fancy any numismatist would give you several sovereigns for it.'

'Numis – thingamajig – who's he?'

'A man who buys and sells old coins.'

'That's enough of the highbrow stuff. What is it, anyway?' demanded Algy shortly.

'I've only seen one once before, and that was in a museum, but I believe I am right in saying that it is a doubloon,' answered Biggles quietly.

Ginger leaned forward, eyes sparkling. 'Great Scott! Those are the things the pirates used to collect, aren't they?'

Biggles nodded. 'The reason being that doubloons were Spanish currency in the days when buccaneers and pirates sailed the seas. Put it in your pocket, Dick – and the letter. I've got an idea that your father's message is going to prove more interesting than you imagined – a lot more. And, to be quite honest, I'd like to have a look at it myself,' he added, as Dick put the coin, and the letter, out of sight.

'Read it, sir, by all means,' invited Dick.

'Not here. Our seafaring friend might be hanging about. We'll go to my rooms, if it's all the same to you.'

'It's all the same to me – better, in fact,' declared Dick. 'But for you I shouldn't have had it.'

'Well, let's finish our sausages and go home,' suggested Ginger. 'I'm fairly aching to see that letter. All my life I've wanted to find a bag of doubloons.'

'A lot of people feel that way,' murmured Biggles.

'Just now you said buccaneers *and* pirates,' ventured Dick, as they resumed their meal with renewed interest. 'What was the difference – was there any?'

'Yes, and no,' answered Biggles. 'The buccaneers came first. When there were more sailors than could find employment, some of them took to a life ashore in the West Indies, where they made a living by killing the animals that had been left behind by the Spaniards on such islands as Hispaniola – the place we now call Haiti. You see, when gold was discovered on the mainland, in Mexico and Peru, the Spaniards who had settled on the island sailed away to see if they could get hold of some of it, and having no means of transporting them, they left their domestic animals behind – cows, pigs, and the like. These ran wild and soon increased in numbers. The out-of-work English and French sailors hunted them, killed them, dried the meat and sold it to the ships that called. They called the stuff *boucan*, which was really the French word for cured beef. So they became known as *boucaniers*, or, in our language, buccaneers, and buccaneers they would have stayed if the Spaniards had had any sense. But they objected to anyone else trading in the New World, and tried to drive the buccaneers, who at that time were perfectly harmless people, out of Hispaniola. They did, in fact, kill a lot of them. Naturally, the buccaneers resented this treatment, to say the least of it; they fought back, and there were some nasty goings-on. In the end the Spaniards won – or it looked that way to them at the time. The buccaneers were driven out, but they didn't go far. They pulled up at a rocky island not far away called Tortuga, where they started thinking about revenge. Not only thinking. They built boats and began making raids against the Spaniards. From that they went to attacking Spanish ships at sea. They fought like fury, and taking the guns from the ships they captured, soon made Tortuga a pretty impregnable fortress. They also constructed forts at other points about the islands.

'What happened after that was a pretty natural consequence,' continued Biggles. 'Rumours of the great quantities of gold being captured from the Spanish galleons got abroad, and the toughest toughs in the world headed for Tortuga to join in the fun. Another colony sprang up at Port Royal, in Jamaica, which must have been a pretty hot spot. The Spaniards now began to get what they'd asked for. The old buccaneering business was forgotten and the one-time buccaneers became pirates pure and simple. They attacked anything and everything anywhere and anyhow. Knowing that if the Spanish caught them they'd be burned, and if the English caught them they'd be hanged, they fought like devils, neither giving nor asking quarter. The Spanish government couldn't shift them, and neither, for that matter, could the British. In the end they were strong enough to take and sack even the largest Spanish cities on the Main. Morgan had eighteen hundred men behind him when he went to Panama.'

'What happened to them at the finish?' asked Dick breathlessly.

'The English government did the only thing it could do. It offered them all a free pardon if they'd turn from their wicked ways. Most of them accepted and either settled down or joined the navy. Morgan, probably the biggest cutthroat of the lot, was knighted by the king and made governor of Jamaica. Knowing all the tricks of the trade, he rounded up and hanged all his old pals who had not accepted the free pardon, so in the course of time the business of piracy fizzled out. The coming of steamships finally put the tin hat on it.'

'Pity,' murmured Dick, with genuine regret.

Biggles smiled. 'So you'd like to be a pirate, you bloodthirsty young rascal, would you?'

'There must have been a lot more fun in it than selling papers at three-ha'pence a dozen.'

'Yes, perhaps you're right,' agreed Biggles, 'although there was nothing funny in swinging on a yard-arm or a gibbet. But if everyone has finished we might as well get along.'

He paid the bill and they passed out into the dreary, lamp-lit street.

Dick opened his mouth to speak, and stepped into the gutter to get beside Biggles just as a heavy lorry swung round the corner.

Algy saw his danger and dragged him aside just in time. The lorry whirled past, missing him by inches.

Biggles eyed Dick seriously. 'My goodness! That was a close squeak,' he breathed. 'You ought to know better than to wander in the road like that.'

Dick turned up a startled face. 'Yes,' he said, thoroughly shaken. 'I can't think what came over me; I never did a thing like that before in my life.'

'Well, don't do it again, or your doubloon won't bring you much luck,' admonished Biggles as, reaching a broad street, he beckoned a cruising taxi.

They got in, and the driver, possibly because he had a long journey before him, set off at high speed. From his position in the rear seat of the cab Biggles regarded the back of the driver's head with strong disapproval. 'This fellow is either mad or drunk,' he declared. 'He has no business to go at this rate; we shall bump into something in a minute, the silly ass.'

'That would be a shame, just as I've come into some money,' protested Dick.

'As far as I can make out, you're going to be lucky if you live long enough to spend it,' muttered Biggles angrily as the taxi skidded round the corner, narrowly missing a stationary dray. 'Open the window, Algy, and tell that fool at the wheel that we didn't ask him to set up a record.'

Algy did as he was asked, but the driver merely laughed as though the whole thing was a joke.

Biggles muttered savagely, and regarded the oncoming traffic with increasing anxiety.

The end came suddenly, at the corner of Mount Street, not far from Biggles's rooms, where the driver swerved to miss a private car that was creeping out of a side street. There was a scream of brakes, and an instant later a sickening crash as the cab struck a traffic signal. Fortunately, it did not turn over.

Biggles was white with anger as he extricated himself from the others on the floor and kicked open the buckled door. 'Anybody hurt?' he asked quickly.

Receiving assurances that no-one was injured, he turned to the driver who, looking thoroughly frightened and ashamed, was wiping the blood from a cut on his forehead with his handkerchief. But before he could speak a policeman appeared, notebook in hand, thrusting his way through the rapidly forming crowd. 'Who did this?' he asked menacingly, pointing to the smashed traffic light.

Biggles nodded in the direction of the driver. 'He did. He drove like a lunatic. He must be drunk,' declared Biggles bitterly.

The driver denied the charge indignantly. 'That ain't

true, sir. I ain't 'ad a drink all day, and that's the 'onest truth, strike me dead if it ain't. You smell my breath if you don't believe me.'

Biggles shook his head. 'No, I don't think I'll do that, thank you. The constable might like to,' he added. There was something in the man's attitude that led him to think that the driver was speaking the truth. 'What on earth made you drive as you did?' he asked.

'I don't know, s'welp me,' declared the wretched man, regarding the ruins of his cab. 'It just seemed as if I couldn't 'elp meself. The funny thing was, I knew I was going too fast, yet I didn't seem able to stop. It was almost as if some one was sitting on the seat beside me saying, "Go on, put your foot down and let her rip." I—'

'All right, that'll do,' put in the constable heavily. 'You come along with me; I'll get the doctor to have a look at you.'

Still protesting volubly, the driver was led away. The others were left standing on the pavement.

'Come on,' muttered Biggles disgustedly. 'We might as well walk the rest of the way. And we'd better insure our lives before we do anything else, I think. That's two narrow escapes inside half an hour. If this sort of thing goes on I shall soon begin to think you're a hoodoo, Dick.'

However, they reached Biggles's flat without further incident, beyond the fact that they all got wet, for it was now raining steadily. They changed their jackets, Ginger lending Dick one of his, and then settled round the fire. Biggles lit a cigarette 'Go ahead, Dick,' he invited. 'Let's hear what your father has to say about the doubloon.'

'I'd rather you read the letter yourself, sir,' suggested Dick nervously. 'My dad didn't write much of a hand, and it always took me a long time to make out the words.'

'All right.' Biggles took the proffered letter. 'I'll read it aloud,' he said, 'then we shall all hear what there is to hear at the same time.' He unfolded several sheets of flimsy paper and smoothed them out on his knee. 'Now then, pay attention, everybody,' he said. 'I'm going to start.'

Chapter 3

The Letter

Dear Dick,

I don't suppose you'll ever get this, but if you do I want you to read it very carefully, and likewise take care of it, because one day it may help you to find a fortune. Yes, a fortune. But don't say nothing to nobody, see, or belike you'll get your throat cut afore you can get yer hands on the dibs. Now then; I'll start at the beginning.

As you know, a finer ship's company you couldn't find than we had in the old *Seadream*, bless her rusty sides. She was a good 'un if ever there was one, and now gone to Davy Jones with most of the good shipmates on her because of that drunken villain Dooch, or Deutch, however he spells his name. A nasty looking man with a round scar at the end of his mouth what don't make him no prettier. But I can't talk about him now because I must get on, having a lot to say.

On this last trip I knew we was in for trouble the minute I clapped eyes on Deutch, who was our new first mate in place of poor Sam Hankin, who was as fine a sailor as ever handled a rope, and knew us all down in the fo'castle like we were his own boys. Sam was sick and Deutch took his place. That was the way of it. And we hadn't sighted the Nab Light when I knew we was in for a dirty trip. Bound for Rio, we was, in ballast, and rolling in a middling north-west gale, we runs down a ketch, making close reefed for port. All because Deutch, who was on the bridge, wouldn't give way, like he ought to have done, us being a steamer. What was worse, we didn't stop. And why? I'll tell you. Deutch was drunk. I needn't say no more about that, but I can tell you there was some funny talk in the fo'castle, as you might guess. In the morning someone tells the skipper, and then the fat was in the fire. Deutch had it in for the lot of us. That was the start.

I needn't tell you about the next fortnight. Deutch made all our lives a hell, and I began to see that if we got to Rio without bloodshed we should be lucky. To make matters worse, the Old Man* slips down the fore companion and lays himself out by knocking his head on a block. And that was how things was when the big blow hits us. Skipper sick, mate drunk, hands grumbling and nothing shipshape. And this, Dick, is where the story really begins.

It ain't no manner of use me trying to tell you just where we was when the hurricane struck us. It ain't for the likes of me to know. But the blow come from the south-east'ard and it tore up such waves as I never see in my life afore. The seas turned into hollow breakers which made the *Seadream* stick her nose into the air, and we began to ship water faster than we could pump it out. The water doused the fires and the mainmast went by the board, taking with it a lot of gear including the wireless, and before long we was drifting as helpless as an old barrel.

For four days we drifted without sighting a ship, and all the time we was leaking like a sieve and getting lower and lower in the water. I tell you, son, me and my shipmates was a pretty miserable lot, what with not having no sleep and exhausted working the hand pumps and knowing as how we couldn't keep afloat much longer.

Presently it was clear that the old *Seadream* would founder any minute, and we see about getting the boats out. None of

* Sailor's slang for the Captain of a ship.

43

us would go without the skipper, so we carries him up and puts him in the first boat. Pity Deutch hadn't been in her, too. There was still a big sea running, and the boat, swinging on the davits as we lurched, smashed to bits, and every soul in her fell into the water and was drowned. Deutch was hanging on a rope just getting into the boat when it happened, but he managed to hold on and claw his way back on deck. There was five of us left all told; me, Deutch, Tom Allen from Pompey, Joe Stevens, the cook, and Charlie Bender, the same Charlie as come 'ome with me once. You remember Charlie, a little fellow with a fair moustache? He come from Gillingham.

Now it ain't no use wasting time telling you about our voyage in the last boat. About a fortnight it was before we sighted land, and how we kept alive, only the Almighty knows. I can't make it out nohow. No, nor how we got to where we did, for our first landfall was an island called Providence in the Caribbean Sea. Deutch and me both knew it by the funny shaped hill at the end, both of us having watered there in the old sailing days. A caution it was how we got there. But before we could set foot on shore a current carried us out to sea again on a new course to the south-west. We hadn't no strength left to pull on the oars, so we had to put up with it. A bitter sight it was to see the land disappearing again, I can tell you, after all we had been through, and us half dead with hunger and thirst. I forgot to tell you that Tom Allen was already dead. Poor Joe died that night. But at last the current took us to another island; and when me, Charlie, and Deutch lands on it, it looks like our troubles was about over, for there was coconuts to eat and milk to drink. I don't know the name of this island. I wish I did, as you will see. But my worst troubles was yet to come.

Deutch's temper now that he couldn't get liquor was awful, and while we was waiting for a boat to pick us up I

44

used to go off by myself looking for grub or watching for a ship. Our island wasn't by any means a little place. As some islands go it might be, but I reckon it was best part of ten miles long by five wide at the widest part, narrowing down at the ends like a new moon. And now there comes a surprise that will sound like a story in a book, but it's true, as you will see from what I enclose in this letter.

One morning, after we had been on the island about a month, Deutch wakes up and curses me for not having water handy. I like a fool ups and tells him that I ain't no lackey, whereupon he comes at me with his knife, and I, not having nothing to defend myself with, runs off with him after me. Soon I comes to a place what I'd seen afore, a sort of dip, or dell-hole, a mossy place filled with bushes and creepers and things, and thinking as how it would make a good hiding place, I jumps into it. I jumped into more than I bargained for, by a long shot, for the ground seemed to open and swallow me up, as they say, and I lands slap in another world. When I opens my eyes I sees as I'm in the saloon of an old fashioned ship like they've got models of in the Museum at Greenwich. I thought for a minute I was dead, or knocked unconscious, with my spirit wandering about in some other place. You see, son, I couldn't make sense of it nohow, because here I was some way from the shore, and how could a ship get there? A ship can't sail over land. So, as I say, I thought as how I'd got knocked silly, and I just lay there waiting to see what was going to happen next. After a time, when nothing does happen, I gets up and begins to wonder if I'm dreaming after all. The things all seemed solid enough, but so quiet you could hear a pin drop. Well, I thinks, this is a rum go, and starts to have a look round. Then I see the hole in the roof where I'd tumbled in, and that sort of gave me an idea of what was what. And now I'll tell you what I saw.

The first thing I claps eyes on give me a rare fright, I can tell you. It was a dead man, although I see at a glance that he'd been dead a long time. It wasn't so much a corpse as a skellington, with the old-fashioned clothes still hanging on the bones, and it fair gave me the creeps to see him sitting there at a big desk grinning out of empty eye-holes at something what lay in front of him.

Presently I plucks up courage to go closer and look at what he was grinning at. There was several things on the desk, and I reckon they are still there, because I didn't touch nothing except what — p'raps you can guess. But I'm going too fast. On the desk there was a big candlestick what looks as if might be silver. Beside it there was an old-fashioned pistol like those you see decorating the walls at the Tower of London. Likewise there was a bit of paper and an old feather sharpened to a point, what I believe the dead man had been using as a pen to write with, because there was writing on the paper, which is the yellow piece I am putting in this letter. But what the pore dead feller seemed to be grinning at was a queer sort of foreign-looking medal. By the weight of it I thinks it's gold. Anyway, thinking as how it might be handy, I slips it in my pocket. Likewise I am sending it to you with the paper, which I can't make head nor tail of, but it struck me it might be a sort of chart marking where there is some money, being as how I couldn't find none, which seemed a bit funny considering the other things I found when I looked round.

I ain't got time to tell you everything I seen in this ramshackle old hulk, but I can tell you I was fair amazed, as you will be if ever you claps eyes on it. There was all sorts of things stored in chests: clothes and silks and satins. Maybe this is what the pore feller was going to hide when he died. As I say, I couldn't work it out nohow, but it's a fair knockout.

When I comes to go I find as I'm in a rare mess, because I couldn't get back up to the hole I'd fell in. You'll laugh when I tell you how I got out. I stove a hole through the bows of the hulk. Rotten they was, like sawdust, but I got out, and had a good look round so as I'd know the place again. And now I'll tell you how to find it if ever you go looking for it, although my bit of a chart what I've made to put in this letter ought to give you the general direction.

The place seems like at some time or other it had been a narrow channel, running up from the sea about a hundred yards from the shore. How the ship got in I can't make out, because there certainly ain't no way out. And when you're out you can't see the ship because she's all overgrown with weeds and things. But there she is, as large as life, with rocks on each side of her. Anyway, I thinks to myself, Deutch shan't know anything about this, I'll share it with Charlie, so I covers up the hole I'd fallen in with some bits of palm so that it couldn't be seen by no one outside, which I reckoned was pretty smart. And then, thinking that Deutch might have quieted down by now, back I goes to the place where we lived, under a piece of overhanging rock by a little lagoon.

Deutch was sitting there as quiet as a lamb, but he gives me a dirty look when I comes up and says I'd better see about the water in future, which I promises to do. And just as I was going to sit down, would you believe it, the golden medal I'd picked up in the ship slips through a hole in my pocket what I'd forgot, and there it lays on the sand as plain as daylight for Deutch to see. 'Where the blazes did you get that?' he cries out, with his eyes fairly popping out of his head, in a manner of speaking. 'That's my business,' I sez boldly, as Charlie picks up the medal to have a look at it. At this Deutch changes his tune. 'Come on, old shipmate,' he sez in a weedling voice. 'We've shared everything up to now. Let bygones be bygones and share and share alike, like good companions everyone.' 'No, Mr Deutch,' I sez. 'Findings keepings. You ain't never shared anything with me, and I ain't parting.' 'Ho, ain't you, you old fool,' he snarls, and before I knew what he was going to be at he comes at me with his knife, which he always kept handy. Charlie, like a good shipmate, jumps in to stop him, and the blade catches him fair in the throat. There he stood, still holding the medal in his hand, making a horrible gurgling noise, with the blood spurting out on the sand. Made me feel fair sick, it did. Then he gives a loud cry, lets go the medal and drops down dead. Like lightning I snatches up the medal and backs away from Deutch, who goes all white and frightened when he sees the dreadful thing he's done. 'That's murder, Mr Deutch,' I hollers, hardly knowing what I was saying. 'I'll report this to the owners when we get back.'

Deutch didn't wait for no more, no more did I. After me he comes and off we go, him cursing, which don't do no man any good. Any fool can curse, but it takes a still tongue to make a wise head, as an old captain of mine used to say. But I was telling you. Somehow I managed to get away, and hid in the woods, where I stayed for the rest of the time I was on the island. Many a time I saw Deutch hunting for the place where I'd found the gold piece, but he never found it and he never found me. And that's how things were when one day the *Portsdown*, an American schooner, puts in for water. I sees her first and went running down to the beach, and then Deutch comes too, only he daren't do anything to me in case the sailors were looking. So when the *Portsdown* sailed we went with her. What a trip it was, too. Everything going wrong all the time. We lost our rudder and a spar fell, killing two men. I haven't time to tell you all about the things that happened on the *Portsdown* while we were aboard her, but at last we comes to Boston where I am now, in fear of my life from Deutch, who told me on the *Portsdown* that unless I told him where I'd found the gold he'd knife me. I shan't tell him, you may be sure.

I'm hoping I shall be lucky enough to work a passage home, so tonight when I leave the hospital I'm going down to the docks. If I can't find a ship I shall give this letter to a sailor homeward bound; then no matter what happens Deutch won't get the gold.

In case anything should happen to me, you try and find the island when you get old enough because I think there is a lot of money hidden there. If not, the things in the old ship should be worth a fair bit. Steer a course for Providence, then swing to the south-west for maybe forty or fifty miles. You can tell the island by high rocky hills on the east side. You'll find the wreck I've marked on the map at the north end, near an islet, which is as near as I can fix it.

You can't tell how much I am looking forward to seeing you again after all this time. Trusting this finds you in better health than I am.

Your affectionate Father

Chapter 4

Biggles Makes a Proposition

There was a full minute's silence after Biggles stopped reading, a silence broken only by the faint rustle as he unfolded a little yellowish slip of paper that had been enclosed in the letter. He gazed at it for some seconds without speaking; then, looking up, he smiled faintly at the intent expressions on the faces of the others. 'Well, so now we know,' he observed quietly.

'You mean — why that sailor was after my letter?' said Dick, quickly.

'Of course.'

'Because he knew that piece of gold was in it?'

Biggles shook his head. 'No, I don't think *that* was what he was after. What *he* wanted to know was where your father found it.'

'So that he could go and get the rest, if there was any?'

'That's more like it.'

'What do you make of it, sir? Do you think that my father really did stumble on to one of these old treasures?'

'I don't think there is any doubt about it. Your father wasn't the sort of man to sit down and make up a tale like that, was he?'

'No, he wasn't, and that's a fact,' declared Dick emphatically. 'He wouldn't do a thing like that.'

'That's what I thought. There is a tone about this letter that makes every word ring true, and there's the coin to prove it.'

'And what's your opinion of it all, sir?' inquired Dick eagerly.

'There's no need to keep calling me "sir",' Biggles told him quietly. 'It looks to me, Dick, as if your father discovered one of the several secret hoards that undoubtedly exist in that part of the world where the pirates did their hunting. There were no banks available, and they had either to carry their ill-gotten gains about with them, or hide them. Inevitably, their ships were often wrecked and all hands drowned, so their secrets died with them – either that, or the money went to the bottom of the sea when their ship foundered. I should say that your father found an old wreck which, through the centuries, has become covered with vegetation; the jungle grows very quickly in the tropics, you know. Wait a minute.' Biggles walked over to the bookcase and took down a heavy encyclopedia. 'Listen to this,' he went on, after he had run quickly through the pages.

'For those who may be sceptical about the vast wealth carried by galleons of this period, the following well-authenticated instance is given. In 1680, a sailor in this country told of a Spanish galleon he had seen lying wrecked on the north-east coast of Hispaniola. Lord Albemarle persuaded Charles the Second to lend him a frigate and he financed an expedition to recover the treasure. It failed. Five years later, another sailor, this time in Jamaica, reported that he had found the wreck with gold and silver lying all around her. Lord Albemarle formed a company and sent out another expedition under a Captain Phips. It returned laden with as much gold as it could carry. Some silver had perforce been left behind. The King received ten per cent of the treasure trove, the value of which exceeded £300,000. Lord Albemarle received £90,000 for his share, and investors of one hundred pounds in the company received £8,000 each.'

'That will give you an idea of the sort of money-boxes that used to float about the high seas in the old days,' observed Biggles. 'When Deutch spotted that doubloon he was cute enough to guess what it might lead to, but your father was too clever for him. Or maybe he wasn't so clever after all, since he did not manage to get back to England, whereas Deutch did.'

Dick started. 'What makes you think that Deutch got back?'

'I imagine it was Mr Deutch who called upon you this afternoon, and with whom we afterwards had a few sharp words. Your father describes just such a scar as was worn by your unpleasant visitor. Surely that can't be coincidence?'

There was another short silence.

'You think he might have killed my dad?' said Dick in a low voice.

'I think it is highly probable. We saw for ourselves how handy he was with his knife, and with such an incentive to murder as treasure, he wouldn't make any bones about using it. I'm sorry, laddie, but it's no use shutting our eyes to the facts, and that's how they look to me.'

'My father was dying in a low dive from a knife wound, so the sailor who brought the letter told me,' muttered Dick chokingly.

Biggles shrugged his shoulders. 'Which all goes to confirm our deductions. Deutch thought probably your father had a map, or something of the sort, and he hoped to get it. To a great extent he was right, because quite apart from the fact that your father may have already drawn the map of the island which he sent home, there was the piece of paper found on the desk on the old ship. But either Deutch was too late, or your father had it too well hidden. Perhaps he had already given it to the sailor to bring home.' A puzzled look came suddenly into Biggles's eyes, and he glanced again at the letter. '*When* did you say the sailor brought the letter to you?' he asked sharply.

'This afternoon.'

'Then he was the dickens of a long time delivering it. This letter is dated nearly three months ago. I wonder why he was so long.'

'He told me about that,' answered Dick quickly. 'They had an awful voyage. At first they ran into gales, then they cast a propeller blade, and then, to finish up with, they had a collision with a trawler coming up the Channel and had to go into a French port for repairs.'

Biggles whistled softly. 'I *shall* begin to think there is something fishy about this business if these tales of trouble go on,' he said half jokingly. 'Well, there it is, Dick. I'm afraid you'll never learn the details of what happened in America after your father wrote this letter. The point is, it has reached you. What are you going to do about it?'

'Hadn't I better go to the police?'

'With what object?'

'To get Deutch run in for murdering my dad.'

'What evidence have you got for making such an accusation? My dear boy, it's one thing to suspect somebody of committing a crime, but quite another matter to prove it. Besides, the affair happened in America.'

'What can I do about it, then?'

Biggles stared thoughtfully into the fire. 'It's a bit hard to know what to advise,' he said slowly. 'Far from looking for Deutch, you'd better keep out of his way. He's far more likely to hurt you than you him. He's still on the trail of the treasure. Somehow, we don't know how, he knows about you. Your father may have mentioned you to him before the trouble started. He might even have discovered that your father wrote a letter to you, in which case he might have sent you the secret. Indeed, I think his actions rather go to prove that. But it is really guesswork. Let us stick to facts. What we do know is this. First, somewhere in the West Indies there is an old hulk, with articles of value, possibly treasure, on board; secondly, there is a nasty piece of work named Deutch prowling about who also knows it; thirdly, he knows you've had a letter because he has held it in his hand; and lastly, but by no means least, he has shown you that he is going to leave no stone unturned to get hold of it. That's all, but it should be enough to convince you that it isn't safe for you to wander about the East End of London by yourself. If you do, as sure as fate Deutch will get hold of that letter and you will come to a sticky end trying to defend it.'

Dick moved uneasily. 'What the dickens can I do?' he asked. 'It looks to me as if I'm in a nice fix. For two pins I'd burn the blessed thing, and tell Deutch what I'd done if he came after me.'

'You don't suppose he'd believe that, do you?'

Dick made a gesture of helplessness. 'No, I don't suppose he would, now I come to think about it. I don't want a knife in my ribs.'

'You haven't said anything about trying to find the treasure,' pointed out Biggles helpfully.

'It wouldn't be much use, would it?' muttered Dick despondently. 'I mean, tuppence wouldn't get me much further than Gillingham, even on a workman's ticket,* much less the West Indies.'

Biggles turned to the others. 'Do you think we might help him?' he suggested.

'Help me!' Dick sprang to his feet, face radiant. 'You mean—'

'We might all go on this treasure hunt.'

* A special cheap ticket for people travelling before a certain hour in the morning by bus or train.

Dick turned pale with excitement. 'Gosh! That would be grand,' he cried. 'When could we start?'

Biggles laughed softly. 'Wait a minute! Wait a minute!' he said lightly. 'You can't just put on your hat and coat and dash off on a trip of this sort. There are a lot of things to be thought of. We've done a bit of travelling in our time, and we know. First of all, there is the question of money; we should need rather a lot.'

'Ah! I was afraid of that!' exclaimed Dick miserably.

'I didn't say that we hadn't got enough,' went on Biggles quickly. 'Look here, Dick. Here's a proposition. Suppose I found the money for this show and we all went with you to collect the doubloons; would you agree to divide the profits into two, you taking one half and we the other, after deducting the cost of the expedition, whatever it may be? That sounds fair to me.'

'It sounds more than fair,' declared Dick promptly. 'I reckon the treasure is as much yours as it is mine. But for you I should have lost the letter and known nothing about it.'

'All right. That's fine. I can see that we shan't fall out over the division of the doubloons – if there are any – in which case all that remains is to make the necessary arrangements for getting hold of them as soon as possible, before Mr Deutch starts any monkey business. But we've got to go to work carefully. Well begun is half done on a job like this. First of all, we've got to locate the island, which may not be as easy as it sounds.'

'What about the map?' put in Algy quickly.

'It only gives the general configuration of the island,' answered Biggles. 'It doesn't give its position. All we know about it is what Dick's father says in his letter, that it is about fifty miles south-west of Providence. There may be several islands. In fact, there are pretty certain to be, because the Caribbean fairly bristles with islands, large and small.'

'What about the paper Dick's father found in the cabin – the one that was lying in front of the skeleton?' put in Algy.

Biggles pursed his lips. 'I'm afraid that isn't going to be much use,' he answered dubiously. 'It looks more like a jigsaw puzzle than a map, although it may take on some sort of meaning when we get to the actual spot. What we've got to do for a start is to find the island; after that, the chart will give us the approximate position of the galleon. I say approximate because I've had some experience of sketch-maps. When the thing that is drawn on this sheet of paper—' Biggles touched the map drawn by Dick's father '—becomes a mass of rock and undergrowth, perhaps a mile or two square, it becomes a different proposition. Take the case of Cocos Island, in the Pacific. It is known for certain that there is at least one treasure there. It isn't a very big island, yet any number of men have searched for years without finding anything more interesting than sand and pebbles. One fellow, a German, lived on the spot for, I think, eighteen years, during which time he dug enough trenches to make a fair-sized battlefield, but all he got for his pains were calloused palms and malaria. But that's by the way. Let's concentrate on getting to the island; we can start looking for the bullion bags when we get there.'

'That suits me,' agreed Dick, optimistically.

'Then we'll have a look at the big atlas in a minute,' resumed Biggles. 'The obvious course seems to be to choose a base as near as possible to the general locality, and then see about getting an aircraft out to it.'

'Did you say *aircraft*?' asked Dick breathlessly.

'I did,' answered Biggles. 'I suppose you were thinking about a ship?'

'Of course; I didn't think of anything else,' admitted Dick.

'I think we can do better than that,' returned Biggles.

'You see, Dick, we all happen to be pilots, so, naturally, when we go anywhere, we fly.'

'That makes it all the better,' cried Dick enthusiastically. 'I've never been in an aeroplane in my life, but I've always wanted to fly.'

'You'll have plenty of flying by the time this business is over, if I know anything about it,' smiled Biggles. 'Get down the atlas, Ginger, and let's have a look at the Caribbean.'

In a moment or two the heavy tome was on the table, open at a double page entitled 'The West Indies and the Caribbean Sea'.

'Now then! Here we are,' murmured Biggles, drawing a rough oval on the map with a lead pencil. 'Here is Providence, the island Dick's father and Deutch saw when they were in the open boat, but on which they could not effect a landing. Instead, they drifted away to the south-west, like this—' Biggles followed a south-westerly course with his pencil '—and here we come to a whole lot of little islands. As you can see, most of them are such mere specks that they wouldn't be shown on an ordinary atlas. Some of them are probably nothing more than cays, which are really only glorified sandbanks. On the other hand, some of them will probably turn out to be a good deal larger than you might suspect from looking at the map. Don't forget that an island of twenty or thirty square miles can only be shown as a dot on a map of this size. But that's by the way. This is the area we have got to explore. I don't think it's any use thinking of trying to make a base among the islands themselves because it would not be possible to get petrol there, or stores. Kingston, Jamaica, is too far away; so is Port of Spain.* But we needn't worry about that. The

* On the island of Trinidad.

nearest island isn't more than a couple of hundred miles from the mainland, a matter of two hour's flight at the very outside, so there should be no particular hardship in flying to and fro. So what we've got to do is choose a town on the mainland where we can get fuel and food.'

'How about Marabina?' suggested Algy.

'I was just looking at it; it ought to suit us admirably; in fact, I don't think we could do better,' replied Biggles.

'Marabina? That's a new one on me,' declared Ginger.

'I've never heard of the place, either,' confessed Dick, who, with the others, was leaning over Biggles's shoulder looking at the atlas.

'It's the capital of one of those funny little countries in Central America, tucked in between Costa Rica and Honduras,' Biggles told him as he closed the book. 'It's on the Pan-American air route to South America, so we ought to have no difficulty in getting petrol there. I expect it's a marine airport; most of them are along that stretch, which means that we shall need a marine aircraft.'

'You mean a seaplane?' asked Dick.

'A flying-boat, probably, or possibly an amphibian,' returned Biggles. 'An amphibian can come down on either land or water. It would be useful to be able to land on a beach, should we find it necessary,' he went on. 'We'll see what we can pick up in America. I've no intention of trying to fly the Atlantic, and I don't think there is any point in going to the expense of shipping a machine across from England. But there, we can settle these details later on. We'll spend the day tomorrow going into the whole thing. Meanwhile, I think it would be a sound scheme if we went out and had a bite of dinner.'

'I was just thinking the same thing,' agreed Algy.

They all got up as Mrs Symes, Biggles's old housekeeper, appeared in the doorway. She turned a reproachful eye on the party. 'How many times have I got to tell you boys to wipe your feet on the front door mat when you come in?' she scolded, half jokingly, half angrily.

Biggles looked up in surprise. 'But we did, Mrs Symes,' he protested. 'I certainly did. We've been in a couple of hours or more, anyway.'

'Well, there now. I wonder who could have made such a mess,' went on the housekeeper. 'One of those young rascals of errand boys, I'll warrant.'

A suspicious look came suddenly into Biggles's eyes. Getting up rather quickly, he walked over to where she was standing and stared down at a number of muddy footmarks on the landing close to the door. In one place there was quite a pool of water. 'It's still raining, isn't it?' he said quietly.

'It's coming down cats and dogs,' declared the housekeeper.

'Humph! That's queer.' Biggles lit a cigarette and then looked back at the floor. 'Sorry we made this mess, Mrs Symes,' he said slowly. 'You'd better clean it up. I'll try not to let it happen again.'

Algy looked at him askance as Mrs Symes went through to her kitchen. 'What's on your mind?' he inquired shrewdly.

'Somebody has been standing outside this door – for some time, too, by the look of it,' murmured Biggles. 'Why do people stand outside doors when other people are inside, talking? Anyone know?'

'To listen to what's being said,' declared Dick promptly.

Biggles nodded sagely. 'That's the answer, Dick. Further, I rather fancy that whoever stood here was wearing oilskins. An ordinary woollen overcoat absorbs water; the outside garment our eavesdropping friend was wearing shot it off on the floor, as you can see. What sort of people wear oilskins besides policemen and postmen, neither of whom are given to keyhole-peeping – not on honest citizens, anyway?'

'Sailors.'

'Right again,' murmured Biggles approvingly.

Dick started as he understood what Biggles was driving at. 'You mean – you think – Deutch followed us here?'

Biggles tapped the ash off his cigarette. 'Come to think of it, there was no reason why he couldn't, if he decided to, was there?' he said quietly. 'You'd better keep close to us, Dick, or we may lose you, and London is a mighty big place to start looking for a small boy with a doubloon in his pocket.'

Chapter 5

Unexpected Difficulties

From five thousand feet Biggles looked down through his windscreen over rolling leagues of sapphire sea, unmarked by a ripple except at the edge, where, in a long line of creamy turquoise, tiny waves lapped idly at the coral strand that meandered mile after mile ahead until at last it lost itself in the purple distance. Beyond it, to the right as the aeroplane flew, stretched the jungle, a vague, monotonous blanket of sombre green that rolled away, fold after fold, to the mysterious shadows of the far horizon.

Beside him, in the second pilot's seat, sat Algy, also gazing ahead, while behind, side by side in the cabin, Ginger and Dick regarded the unchanging scene with the bored disinterest that comes from familiarity.

Nearly a month had elapsed since the discussion in Biggles's rooms. For Dick it had been a period of eager anticipation and delight; for the others, hard work and preparation. It had taken them a fortnight to clear up their affairs and make the necessary arrangements in London, which had included the acquisition of the necessary passports, visas, and carnets.*

---

* A private aeroplane cannot just travel about the world from country to country as some people suppose. Before flying over a foreign country a pilot must first obtain permission in writing from the Government of that country. It will be understood, therefore, that when several countries are involved, the preparations for a long-distance flight are often a tedious and tiresome process, although the aero clubs of the countries concerned do their best to expedite permits and provide facilities. WEJ

Nearly a week had been spent crossing the Atlantic, and then several more days of bustle and anxiety in the United States while Biggles sought an aircraft suitable for their purpose.

In the end he had selected a Sikorsky amphibian, four-seater, twin-engined monoplane with a large luggage compartment, and with this he professed himself satisfied. And so far his opinion had been justified, for the machine had not given them a moment's anxiety since they had taken off, four days previously, on their long run southward, progress being facilitated by the officials of Pan-American Airways – the Imperial Airways of America – whose far-flung system they had obtained permission to use. The only piece of additional equipment they had acquired was a collapsible rubber boat, which Biggles had insisted on taking in case of an emergency landing.

As far as Dick was concerned, four long days in the air had removed all novelty from that mode of travel, and he was looking forward to the time when he would be able to stretch his legs in a sandy cove similar to those they had so often passed, and bathe in the warm, limpid waters of the tropic sea. He knew that according to Biggles's calculations they might reach their objective at any time now, so he was not surprised when presently the roar of the engine died away and the nose of the machine tilted downward. By craning his neck he could just see a large cluster of white, flat-roofed houses, which he knew from the shape of the harbour they skirted was their destination. He caught Ginger's eye and grinned. 'We're there!' he called cheerfully.

Ginger smiled back, nodding. 'Looks like Marabina,' he said, for after some discussion they had finally settled on their original choice as a base from which to work.

'I wonder what sort of a place it is?'

Ginger shrugged his shoulders. 'Much like the other places we've stopped at, except that it is smaller. It's nearer the Equator, so it will certainly be hotter,' he concluded, as the boat-like hull of the amphibian cut a white line of foam across the placid surface of the bay that formed the harbour.

The machine came to rest, rocking gently on an invisible swell. Biggles stood up and folded back the glass cockpit cover. 'That must be Pan-American's moorings, over there,' he said, pointing to a slipway and a wide-mouthed hangar at the water's edge, near which a flying-boat was riding at anchor. 'They told me in New York that this was one of the depots where they keep a spare machine for emergencies. We'll go over there, I think, and tie up by the slipway.'

He was about to sit down again in order to put the plan into execution when a small motor-boat put off from the quay farther down and came chugging towards them; an official in a gaudy but sadly dilapidated uniform stood in the bows, holding up his right hand.

'I think that chap is signalling to us, isn't he?' said Algy dubiously, with his eyes on the boat.

'I believe he is,' replied Biggles standing up again. 'Yes; it's us he's after. I suppose he's coming to have a look at our papers. What's all the hurry, I wonder?'

The boat pulled up alongside the amphibian, the official, a pompous-looking little man, making dramatic signals to the airmen, at the same time firing out a stream of words.

'*No comprendo*,*' said Biggles, who knew a little Spanish, but not enough to keep pace with the present situation.

'I think he means that we are to go with him,' ventured Algy, who was trying to follow the signals.

* Spanish: I don't understand.

Biggles pointed towards the tumble-down landing-stage from whence the boat had appeared, at the same time raising his eyebrows questioningly.

'*Si, si,*' called the official peremptorily.

'That's it,' observed Biggles quietly. 'Pity about that. I'd rather have gone over to the Pan-American people, but apparently we shall have to leave that until later. We had better go with this fellow or we may get into trouble. The smaller the place the bigger idea the officials have of their importance; at least, that's my experience.'

While they had been speaking Biggles had opened the throttle slightly, and had followed the boat to the landing-place where the usual small crowd of loungers were watching the proceedings from behind half a dozen rifle-armed policeman, or soldiers; they might have been either.

'Something tells me that I am not going to like this place,' observed Biggles drily, as he switched off the engine and threw a quick glance at the policemen.

'Why not?' asked Algy sharply, as he made the amphibian fast by the bows.

'I don't know, but there is something in the attitude of those fellows with the rifles that warns me that we shall have to be careful,' answered Biggles. 'I can feel a sort of hostility in the air.'

'Our papers are all in order, so I don't see that we have anything to worry about,' put in Ginger carelessly.

'You might, if you knew as much about these people as I do,' Biggles told him shortly. 'The predatory instincts of their forefathers, the Brethren of the Coast, still breaks out at the slightest excuse. But there, we shall see,' he concluded moodily as he collected all the papers they would be likely to require and prepared to step ashore.

* Spanish: Yes, yes.

'Hadn't somebody better stay here to look after the boat?' inquired Ginger. 'We don't want to get our stuff pinched.'

'They'll want us all ashore for Customs regulations and passport examination,' replied Biggles. 'Come on; you have to take chances and hope for the best in this part of the world. The gentleman in the natty uniform is getting impatient.'

Slowly, for the sun was blazing down fiercely on the exposed wharf, they followed the officer up a flight of ramshackle stairs, and then across a badly kept road to a flight of steps that led upwards towards a stone building standing on a knoll overlooking the harbour.

'Where the dickins is he taking us, I wonder?' muttered Biggles anxiously, eyeing the building towards which they were advancing with disfavour.

'It looks to me more like a prison than anything else,' suggested Algy.

'I was thinking the same thing,' declared Biggles. 'Customs offices are usually on the waterfront, for obvious reasons.'

Still, the official in whose charge they were, approached the building, so they could do nothing but follow, and in a few minutes they were guided through a beautifully carved doorway, evidently a relic of the old colonial days, into a well-furnished office, where a swarthy, cadaverous-looking man, with two armed policemen in attendance, awaited them.

Biggles raised his solar topee courteously. '*Buenos diaz, señor*,*' he greeted pleasantly.

The other returned the greeting, rather coldly, and held out a dirty hand for the documents Biggles tendered. He gave the four travellers a long, searching scrutiny, and then, with irritating slowness, turned over the pages of their passports.

* Spanish: Good day, Sir.

65

'Do you speak English?' Biggles asked him, quite nicely. The man at the desk took no notice.

Biggles glanced at the others. 'In a case like this the great thing is to keep one's temper,' he said, *sotto voce*. 'I have an increasing suspicion that this fellow is going to be awkward.'

Slowly the minutes ticked by. Algy yawned. Ginger began to fidget. Biggles stood quite still, waiting, knowing only too well the folly of trying to hurry matters.

At last the man at the desk looked up and said something sharply in Spanish.

'What did he say?' asked Algy.

'I'm not sure, but I believe he's telling us that there is something wrong with our papers,' answered Biggles, walking nearer to the desk.

Thereafter followed a long conversation, the official, regardless of Biggles's halting Spanish, pouring out a stream of words every time he spoke. At length Biggles shrugged his shoulders helplessly and turned to the others. 'As far as I can make out, he says there should be another paper which we haven't got.'

'What are we going to do about it?' asked Algy.

The question was soon answered. The official said something to Biggles, and then gave an order to the two policemen, who turned towards the door.

'He says it will be quite all right, but we shall have to wait,' explained Biggles. 'Meanwhile we're to go with these fellows. Come on, it's no use kicking; resistance will only make matters worse.'

They all trooped out behind the policemen and followed them up a flight of stairs to a white-washed room, unfurnished except for three or four wooden forms that stood against the walls. The door was closed; a key grated in the lock and they found themselves alone.

Algy looked at Biggles questioningly. 'What's the big idea, do you think?'

'I don't know,' replied Biggles slowly. 'I can't quite make out what's going on. I'm prepared to swear that our papers are in order, and that the hatchet-faced gentleman downstairs knows it, but he's got some reason for holding us up. I can tell it by his manner. Maybe he's just looking for an excuse to charge us with some technical offence as a ready means of making us pay a fine which will probably go into his pocket. If that's the case, the sooner he says so the better. It's usually a matter of money. Half these fellows live on graft – not that one can altogether blame them, because it's their only source of income.'

'I'd see him to the dickens before I'd stand for being blackmailed,' protested Ginger indignantly.

Biggles smiled sadly. 'In these little tinpot states, particularly in Central and South America, the best policy is to pay up and look pleasant,' he said evenly. 'Otherwise it only costs you more in the end, to say nothing of the delay. Still, I must say I don't like the idea of being locked in, or of that window over there being barred.'

They all sat down to pass the time as well as they could. The room was like an oven in spite of the open, iron-barred window, overlooking the harbour, from which they could clearly see the amphibian, less than a quarter of a mile away.

'What about asking to see the British Consul?' suggested Algy. 'There should be one here, I imagine.'

'There will be a Vice-Consul, anyway,' replied Biggles, 'but I don't think it would be wise to mention him at this stage. We don't want to put their backs up. If the worst comes to the worst we shall have to do that, of course.'

An hour passed slowly, another, and another. The sun began to sink behind the jungle-clad hills. A little cloud of mosquitoes appeared and circled slowly in the centre of the room.

Algy suddenly jumped up from the form on which he had

been lying. 'Dash this for a joke,' he snorted wrathfully. 'I've had about as much as I'm going to stand. Anyone would think that we were a bunch of crooks instead of bona-fide travellers. Come on, Biggles, let's raise a stink.'

Biggles got slowly to his feet. 'Yes, I've had about enough of it myself,' he admitted, strolling over to the window. As he looked out the others saw his manner change. His body stiffened. 'What the devil's going on down there?' he cried, pointing towards the amphibian, about which a number of police were standing. One had just emerged from the cabin carrying a bundle. 'Of course, it may only be the Customs people doing their job,' he went on, 'but I don't like the idea of people prowling about our machine when we're not there. I'm going to demand an explanation.'

He walked quickly towards the door, but before he reached it, it was opened from the far side, and no fewer than six policemen entered. With them were the two officials, the one who had met them in the boat, and the other who had examined their passports.

'What is the meaning of all this?' demanded Biggles harshly.

A policeman laid his hand on Algy's arm, but he shook it off angrily.

'All right, take it easy, Algy,' Biggles told him quickly. 'It's no use starting a rough house; we shall only come off worse in the end.'

The passport officer came forward. His manner when he spoke to Biggles was polite, almost obsequious.

'What's going on?' asked Algy, controlling his temper by an effort.

Biggles shook his head helplessly. 'This fellow says that an American aeroplane has been stolen, and as we may have taken it we must submit to being searched.'

'I'll see them frizzling in Hades first,' choked Algy

passionately. 'I've never heard of such a thing in my life. Why don't you demand to see the Consul?'

'I have.'

'What did they say?'

'He isn't here. He has had the fever, and has gone up to the mountains for a change of air.'

Algy swallowed hard. 'I believe the whole thing is a racket,' he grated through set teeth.

Biggles smiled wanly. 'Of course it is,' he agreed. 'The point is, what can we do about it? We can kick up a row when we get back home, but that doesn't help us now, does it? I hate the idea of being searched as much as you do, but, frankly, I don't see that we are in any condition to prevent it. If once we give them an excuse to clap us into jail, we might languish here for months.'

'We made a pretty smart choice of a base, didn't we?' sneered Algy sarcastically.

'I agree, but it's a bit late to think about changing it. Regrets won't get us anywhere. We'd better submit. Luckily, most of my money is in letters of credit and travellers' cheques, so they won't be able to rob us of much.'

After that they submitted to the indignity of being searched, a proceeding that was carried out very thoroughly. Everything was taken from their pockets, including the map of the island and Dick's doubloon. The things were put in a bag and taken away, and again the airmen found themselves alone.

Biggles and Dick alone retained their equanimity. Algy was livid with rage, while Ginger sat on a form and made threats that he was quite powerless to carry out. 'Did you ask that lean-faced swine what his stiffs were doing in our machine?' he challenged Biggles.

'What was the use?' replied Biggles coolly. 'My dear boy, it's no use going off at the deep end. Ill-advisedly, not that we were to know better, we have put ourselves in the clutches of these sharks, and all we can do is sit tight until we get out. Don't think that I am going to let them get away with it. I'm not. But this is neither the time nor place to start threatening.'

'What about my doubloon – and the map?' asked Dick anxiously.

'What about them?' returned Biggles. 'One can only hope that they do not realize their significance. Your doubloon might simply be a souvenir. The map may mean anything. After all, as aeroplane pilots, there is nothing surprising about our being in possession of a map. I've usually got one of some sort on me. In any case, we couldn't have stopped them from taking them with the rest of our things; to have protested would only have called attention to them and aroused suspicion. Don't think I wasn't sorry to see them go out of our possession, but by saying nothing I hoped that they wouldn't attach any particular importance to them.'

'But suppose they *were* sharp enough to connect the doubloon and the map?' insisted Dick plaintively.

But Biggles did not answer. He was standing by the window gazing down at the road that wound round to the harbour. Slowly, an expression of utter incredulity crept over his face.

'What is it?' asked Algy sharply, sensing disaster.

'The answer, I fancy, to the circumstances of our peculiar reception here,' replied Biggles tersely. 'Take a look and see who's walking down the path with our officious friend of the cadaverous face.'

Algy ran to the window. As he looked in the direction indicated his eyes grew round with wonder. 'Heavens!' he breathed. 'It's Deutch!'

Biggles laughed bitterly. 'Astonishing though it may appear, I'm afraid you're right,' he said quietly. 'So now we know. That makes everything as clear as daylight.'

'But how in the name of goodness did *he* get here?' asked Ginger.

Biggles thrust his hands deep into his trousers pockets and bit his lower lip thoughtfully. 'I must admit that such a possibility as his arrival here did not for one instant cross my mind,' he confessed.

'But how did he know we were coming here?' argued Algy.

'You haven't by any chance forgotten the puddle outside our door in London, have you?' inquired Biggles. 'We suspected an eavesdropper, you remember. We even suspected that it was Deutch. He must have heard us decide on this place as a base and got here before us, which accounts for the fact that we saw no more of him in London, a circumstance which struck me at the time as odd. Very clever of him. It looks as if we have made the old and often fatal mistake of underestimating the calibre of our man. We shall know better in future. He got here ahead of us and has apparently managed to get on the right side of the not-too-particular people who run the place. As a sailor, he has probably been here before. Goodness knows what he has told them about us, but whatever it is you may be sure that it's no good. In short, Mr Blessed Deutch has rather upset our carefully loaded applecart.'

'But what about the map and the letter?' cried Algy aghast. 'I'll warrant he's got them by now.'

'He hasn't got the letter because, having committed to memory the rather meagre sailing directions, I left it where, in the event of our non-return, it will be handed over to Colonel Raymond at Scotland Yard, who might one day use it as evidence against friend Deutch.'

'But the map?' cried Algy again.

'A fat lot of use that will be to him.'

'What do you mean?'

Biggles permitted a slow smile to spread over his face. 'I

think you will agree that an incorrect map is worse than no map at all, since it leads one in the wrong direction. You see,' he explained, 'once I suspected that the astute Mr Deutch had followed us home in London, and always taking into consideration the possibility of his getting hold of the map – which, obviously, was what he wanted – I took the precaution of making certain alterations which, while of a minor nature, not only destroys its value, but makes it definitely misleading. Mr Deutch has been clever, but not quite clever enough. He thinks he's won the first round. Has he? We shall see.'

'And in the meantime, what are we going to do about it?' inquired Algy.

'Bar breaking out of this place, which seems to be a rather formidable proposition besides being of questionable wisdom, I don't see that we can do anything except sit here and wait for the next move,' murmured Biggles.

'What! Do you think they'll keep us here all night?' inquired Ginger angrily.

'I shouldn't be surprised,' replied Biggles calmly. 'Now that Mr Deutch has got what he wanted, they will probably keep us here until he gets a good start and then let us go.'

In which supposition Biggles was nearer the truth than he imagined, but not for one instant did he suspect how Deutch's good start was to be achieved.

Little more was said. As the sun sank behind the jungle the sky turned swiftly from azure to egg-shell blue, and then to ever-darkening purple. Night came, and with it the heavy silence of the tropics. Wondering what the morning would bring, the prisoners settled themselves down to pass the night in the least uncomfortable positions they could find.

Chapter 6

Tragic Events

Fluted bars of soft mother-of-pearl light were filtering through the window when Biggles awoke with a start. He was on his feet in an instant. 'Hark!' he cried, as the others sat up in various degrees of wakefulness.

Vibrant on the still air came the roar of aero engines.

'It's only the Pan-American machine getting ready to take off,' declared Algy, settling back again with a yawn.

Biggles darted to the window. 'Pan-American my foot!' he cried. 'It's our machine!'

The others rushed to the window and stared down at the Sikorsky, which was taxi-ing slowly towards the mouth of the harbour, leaving two ever-widening ripples in its wake.

'What the dickens are they going to do with her?' muttered Ginger.

'Perhaps they are just getting the Pan-American people to move her across to the other side out of the way, to make room for a ship, or something,' suggested Algy optimistically.

'Don't you believe it,' snapped Biggles. 'That machine is being taken out of the harbour.' His face was pale as he strode to the door and began beating a rapid tattoo on it with his fists.

Somewhat to his surprise, it was opened almost at once, by a policeman who was evidently just coming in with their breakfasts, for he carried a tray on which was a jug, some cups, a loaf of bread and some fruit. Biggles brushed him aside, as he did two others who tried to stop him, and dashed out of the building and down the road that led to the wharf. But by the time he got there the machine was in the air, so after watching it impotently for a moment or two, he turned about, and with the others close behind, made for the Pan-American hangar, outside which two or three white-clad figures were standing watching the amphibian. The Americans turned to face the airmen as they ran up.

'Did you fellows see who was in that machine?' cried Biggles, waiving formalities.

'Sure,' answered one, a cheerful looking youth, evidently one of the company's mechanics, for the well-known 'flying wing' trademark was embroidered on the breast of his overalls. 'That's your ship, isn't it?' he added.

'It is,' returned Biggles tersely.

'That's what I told my buddy here,' went on the mechanic. 'I watched you bring her in yesterday. I saw you go ashore. Why didn't you come down here to re-fuel, instead of carrying the gas all the way to the wharf?'

Biggles stared. 'Carry the gas?' he echoed in tones of astonishment. 'What do you mean? We haven't had a chance to refuel yet.'

'Your ship was filled up last night by a bunch of guys who carried the stuff from our depot to the wharf.'

Biggles breathed heavily. 'They took our papers and held us on a trumped-up charge of irregularity,' he said bitterly. 'It looks as if we've been swindled out of our machine.'

The other nodded sympathetically. 'Yeah! I guess you've been framed.'

Another of the Americans laughed, but there was no humour on his face. 'These skunks'd frame a mosquito for its hide,' he drawled. 'Looks like you're in a jam.'

'We are,' agreed Biggles crisply. 'I was prepared to be robbed, but I didn't think they'd dare to go so far as to steal an aeroplane. Who took her, boys?'

'Feller named Deutch and his partner. Anyway, Deutch was one of 'em. I saw him get in.'

Biggles caught his breath. 'But he's not a pilot,' he said wonderingly.

'No, but there's a guy with him who is, according to what he says, although I ain't seen his ticket. Deutch blew in here about a week ago with a guy named Harvey, asking about a machine. Harvey claimed that he could fly, and it looks like he told the truth.'

Biggles moistened his lips. 'What have they been doing since they came here?'

'Search me. They rolled up here together asking about hiring a ship, but when the boss asked to see the colour of their money they sheered off. I've seen them once or twice in the town with Mallichore, which was all I needed to put me wise that they were crooks.'

'Who's Mallichore?'

'The Chief of Police. That's his official title. He's the big cheese here, runs the whole burg.'

'Do you mean a cadaverous looking fellow with a yellow skin?'

'That's the boy. You wanna keep clear o' him. He's bad medicine.'

'I'd have kept clear of him had I known what sort of a shark he was, you can bet your life on that,' returned Biggles with bitter emphasis. 'Did anyone see how many people got into my machine?'

'Yeah,' chipped in another mechanic who had appeared from the direction of the wharf while Biggles was speaking. 'There was Deutch, his boozy looking pal Harvey, 'Frisco Jack and Martinez.'

Biggles stared. ''Frisco Jack – Martinez! Who the dickens are they?' he jerked out.

'Good company for the other two,' declared the mechanic who had just spoken. ''Frisco Jack was one of Slick

Ferrara's boys in New York. He bolted here when the cops put him on the spot for plugging one of them. There ain't no extradition here, so he can sit pretty. He runs a dive on the waterfront; he still packs a gun under his armpit, and he knows how to use it, so you'd be a sucker to start anything against him unless you had a machine-gun trained on him first.'

'And the other fellow – Martinez?'

'Pedro Martinez! He's a black guy, besides which I guess he's just about the slimiest thug who walks on two legs. He's Mallichore's bumper-off – does all his dirty work for him. The folks around here say he carries a razor in each pocket, and I guess they oughta know. A guy up on the hill told me he's cut more throats than there are fish in the sea, and if ever you catch sight of him you won't find it hard to believe that. Everyone here's scared stiff of him. If he's in your ship you can bet that Mallichore is in on the deal, whatever it may be.'

'Sounds a nice little party,' observed Biggles in a hard voice.

'As nice as you'd find between Rio and l'il old New York.'

Biggles thought swiftly. Out of the corner of his eyes he could see several armed police running down the hill, and he was in no doubt as to their mission. 'Is your boss about?' he asked.

'Sure. Here he comes now. This is the Superintendent. The name's Timms. You can bet on him for a square deal.'

Biggles turned quickly to meet a broad, cheerful-looking, thick-set man in spotless white ducks* who was coming towards them. 'Good morning,' he said. 'I've just had my ship stolen.'

The Superintendent made a grimace. 'Well, say!' he

---

* White clothes worn in the tropics.

76

ejaculated. 'I saw her take off. Got me guessing when I saw you standing here.'

Biggles nodded. 'I'm not letting them get away with it,' he said grimly. 'Have you got radio equipment here?'

'Sure.'

'Good,' went on Biggles quickly. 'Then just listen to this, because I can see a bunch of trouble coming down the hill. My name's Bigglesworth. You can check up on it. We're a private party cruising the Islands, and the ship you just saw take off is mine. I bought it off your people at Floyd Bennet Field last week. They'll confirm that. There are fifty thousand dollars standing to my credit in the bank on which I drew the cheque. My letters of credit and cheque book have been taken off me, but I'm going to fetch them in a minute. I want another machine. What about the one you've got here? I'm open to buy it outright, or take it on charter, whichever way you prefer.'

The American looked serious. 'I daren't let you have this one,' he said slowly. 'She's our reserve ship.'

'Yes, I know that. How far away is the next one?'

'Maracibo.'

'They could fly it down here in a day, if you needed a spare.'

'Mebbe.'

'Will you get in touch with your people right away and see what you can do? I'm going up to get my things now, then I'll be back. If your people say I can have the ship, fill up the tanks and start her up. I may be in a hurry. I'll bring the cheque with me.'

'OK. I'll do my best.'

'And as we haven't had anything to eat for about twenty-four hours, if you could get a bit of grub aboard—'

The Superintendent waved his hand. 'Leave it to me,' he cried. 'Watch how you go.'

'Thanks!' Biggles turned to face the party of police, or

soldiers, who had now arrived on the scene. With them was the man in the tawdry uniform who had met them in the motor-boat, and he indicated in no uncertain manner that they were to return with him forthwith. Biggles needed no second invitation. His mouth was set in a hard line as, with the others behind him, he set off up the hill. Reaching the stone building, without stopping he strode straight through to the inner office.

Mallichore was sitting at his desk, but he started up as the airmen burst in, with the police at their heels. 'Listen, you,' snapped Biggles harshly, in English. 'I've stood for about as much as I'm going to stand from you. My friends below are already sending a radio message through to the British Foreign Office for me. Get that? The British Foreign Office! I want my things – where are they?'

Mallichore evidently understood, or gathered from Biggles's manner what he meant, for he pointed to the desk on which were piled the things that had been taken from their pockets. He spoke quickly in Spanish, shrugging his shoulders and waving his hands melodramatically.

'What does he say?' asked Ginger.

'Just what I expected he would. He's full of apologies now. Says he's very sorry indeed about the delay, but it is the usual procedure here.'

'Ask him if it's usual for people to have their ships stolen,' growled Algy.

'That won't bring ours back, will it? Pah! What's the use of arguing with the swine? He knows what's happened as well as we do, and he knows we know, but it won't do any good to talk about it. Let's get out. If we can have the Pan-American machine we'll find another base, if we have to go as far as the Bermudas.'

As he spoke, Biggles began picking up the things from the desk and handing them to their respective owners. At last nothing was left. 'Anyone lost anything?' he asked.

'My doubloon,' replied Dick. 'The dirty hound has pinched my doubloon.'

'I thought the sight of a piece of gold would be too much for him,' muttered Biggles. 'I've got everything except the map, not counting a hundred dollar bill that has been taken out of my notecase. I don't think it's any use fighting about it. The sooner we are out of this the better.'

He had half turned towards the door when Dick caught him by the arm. 'Look!' he said. 'There's my doubloon, under the glass.'

Biggles followed the direction of his eyes and saw the coin lying as Dick had described it. It was as if Mallichore had been in the act of examining it when the others had made their abrupt entry, and he had pushed it hurriedly out of sight – as he thought.

Vicious irritation surged through Biggles at the paltry theft. With his eyes on the coin, he took a quick pace forward and stretched out his hand to pick it up, but Mallichore was too quick.

'Why, you dirty crook!' snarled Biggles. Losing his temper and clenching his fists, he took a flying leap over the desk to get at the thief.

'Look out!' Algy yelled the warning.

Biggles snatched a quick glance over his shoulder and saw the muzzle of a rifle pointing at him. He leapt aside just in time. With a deafening roar, intensified by the enclosed area, the weapon exploded. The reek of cordite flooded the room.

In the silence that followed the distant lapping of the waves against the wharf could be heard distinctly. But no-one noticed it. All eyes were on Mallichore. His face was ashen. For perhaps two seconds he stood erect, hand pressed to his breast, while a scarlet blot widened beyond his fingers. Then he fell headlong, with a crash that shook the room. The coin flew from his fingers and spun, a gleaming streak of gold, across the desk. Biggles whipped it up just as it was going to fall to the floor. 'Come on,' he snapped. 'They'll blame us for this.'

As they all made for the door the officer tried to stop them, but Algy hurled him aside. The policeman who had fired the fatal shot was too horrified to move, but another threw up his weapon. Before he could fire it Biggles's fist had caught him on the point of the jaw and sent him spinning into a corner. 'Don't stop for anything,' he snapped, as he slammed the door behind him and took the steps three at a time.

The run down the hill was something none of them will forget. The sun was now high in the sky and the heat was terrific. Occasional pedestrians stared at them, and one or two, apparently connecting them with the uproar that had broken out at police head-quarters, moved as if to stop them, but their courage failed when it came to facing the determined onslaught of the airmen.

'Look!' yelled Biggles exultantly, and the others, following the direction of his outstretched finger, saw the propellers of the flying-boat flashing as they ticked over in the bright sunlight.

They arrived panting. The Americans were grinning. 'Good work, boys,' cried the Superintendent approvingly.

'What about the machine?' gasped Biggles. 'We're in a hurry.'

'Yeah, I noticed it. She's an old ship, so the firm say you can have her for ten thousand bucks, or you can take her on charter at two hundred and fifty a day, you're to pay insurance and leave five thousand deposit.'

Biggles barely heard the end of the sentence. He was writing out a cheque with his fountain-pen faster than he had ever written before, for a full score of police were pelting down the hill.

'OK,' said the Superintendent, glancing at the cheque.

Biggles ran to the machine. The others were already aboard. 'What range have I got?' he called to the chief mechanic.

'A thousand miles.'

Biggles dropped into the pilot's seat as a bullet whistled through the plane. There was a peculiar smile on his face as he groped for the throttle. The engines roared. The nose swung round in a smother of milky foam. The machine surged forward, cutting a clean V-shaped ripple in the water. He jerked the stick back; the keel unstuck, and the flying-boat rose gracefully into the air. 'Phew!' he breathed, with a sidelong glance at Algy. 'I'm glad to be out of that hole.'

'Same here,' agreed Algy. 'I don't think we had better come back this way.'

'We shan't, not if I can prevent it,' declared Biggles grimly.

Chapter 7

The Hurricane

The new aircraft was a pure flying-boat; that is to say, it was not fitted with a land undercarriage. It was larger than their own machine, having accommodation for eight passengers, but being designed for commercial work, the pilot's compartment was separated from the cabin by a bulkhead, although communication could be established by means of a small doorway, the door itself having a glass panel in it through which passengers could, if they wished, see into the cockpit. All of which was, of course, orthodox design in that class of aircraft. It was not the machine Biggles would have chosen in the ordinary way, but he had had no choice, and in the circumstances he accounted himself extremely fortunate in being able to acquire an aircraft of any sort.

He set the machine on a course for the approximate position of the island, and then told Algy to take over control. 'Keep her as she goes,' he ordered. 'We'll put her down at the first decent anchorage we see and have a council of war. Keep your eyes open for the other machine. Deutch must know pretty well where the island is, although he doesn't know the position of the wreck, so if we see our machine on the water near an island it will be fairly safe to assume that it's the one we're looking for.'

'Suppose we spot it, what then?' inquired Algy. 'Are we going down to tackle them?'

'We will go down, but without weapons we're in no case to tackle anybody. I'm hoping the island will be large enough for us to choose a mooring of our own, without our being seen. Even if they see us – or what is more likely, see the machine – there is no reason why they should assume we are in it. I think they will be more likely to take the machine for what it really is, a Pan-American airliner, on routine service.'

'True enough,' agreed Algy. 'We're doing a hundred and forty, so in about an hour or a little more we should make a landfall at the group of islands we looked at in the atlas.'

'That's right. I'd take her up a bit higher, I think; the higher we are the farther we shall be able to see. Level her out at around eight thousand.'

'OK,' acknowledged Algy. 'What are you going to do?'

'I'm going through to the cabin to have a look round. I asked Timms to try to get some food aboard; I hope he managed it, because if I don't soon have something to eat I shall pass out.'

Biggles opened the bulkhead door and went through into the cabin where Ginger and Dick smiled a welcome. But he was not so interested in them as he was at what rested on the table between them. The American had not overlooked his request for food, although there was nothing particularly outstanding about it. A loaf of bread, a piece of cheese, a pot of jam, and a large bunch of bananas made up the total, and although in their hungry condition they might have wished for more, it was enough to satisfy their immediate cravings.

'Take a banana or two out to Algy,' Biggles told Ginger. 'He can eat them as he flies. I'll go and relieve him as soon as I've had a bite.' He broke a piece off the loaf, cut a slice off the cheese with his penknife, and sat down in an empty seat.

'I'm glad you managed to save my doubloon,' said Dick, helping himself to another banana.

'I'd forgotten all about it,' declared Biggles, feeling in his pocket. 'Here you are, you'd better have it.' He took the coin from his pocket and passed it over.

As Dick stretched out his hand to take it a remarkable thing happened. The aircraft soared high, as if it had encountered a colossal up-current, and then dropped like a stone for a good two hundred feet. So violent was the bump when they struck solid air again that Biggles was thrown out of his seat, the bread going in one direction and the cheese in another. Ginger, who was just coming back into the cabin, hurtled inside as if he had been thrown in, and came to rest in a sitting position on the floor with a comical expression of surprise on his face.

'What the dickens was that?' he gasped.

Dick clasped his stomach. 'Crikey!' he breathed. 'Another bump like that and I shall be sick. I feel as if I've left my inside up in the air somewhere.'

Biggles had hurried through to the cockpit. 'Everything all right?' he asked Algy, who threw him a mystified glance.

'Everything's all right as far as I can see.'

'What caused that bump?'

'I don't know. There was absolutely nothing to account for it, not even a cloud. I wasn't ready for it, and it nearly threw me out of my seat. I came to the conclusion that you were up to something in the cabin and had accidentally fouled the controls.'

'No; I was just passing Dick's doubloon over to him,' asserted Biggles. A puzzled expression suddenly crossed his face, but it gave way just as quickly to a smile of derision.

'What's the joke?' asked Algy.

'Nothing much. It just struck me that Dick's doubloon seems to be a hoodoo.'

'Hoodoo?'

'Well, it hasn't been exactly lucky for the people who have owned it, has it? Every time the confounded thing comes to light something seems to happen, like that bump just now.'

'You're not going to ask me to believe that an old coin can have any effect on natural causes, are you?'

'Of course not. It does seem funny, though, doesn't it? First of all there was the ship in which it was found. Something unpleasant happened to that, or it wouldn't be where it is. Something unpleasant also happened to the chap in the cabin, the skeleton Dick's father talked about in his letter. Apparently he died with his boots on. Then there was Charlie, who was with Dick's father and Deutch on the island. He died a sudden death. Dick's father had the coin next, and it didn't do *him* much good, either. Then look at the things that happened to the ship that brought the coin to England. It cast a propeller-blade and was involved in a collision. Before the coin had been in Dick's possession for a day he nearly shared his father's fate, and might have done so had we not appeared on the scene. Half an hour later, with the coin in his pocket, he was nearly run over. On the way home our taxi crashes – a thing that has never happened to us before. Mallichore steals the coin from us, and gets plugged before the day is out! Call it coincidence, call it what you like, but you can't get away from the fact that no less than four men, to our certain knowledge, who have touched the coin have all died sudden deaths. I'm not superstitious, but there is no denying that there have been cases where a sort of evil luck, or fate, has clung to certain objects, and this confounded coin seems to be one of them. Frankly, I don't mind telling you that I shouldn't shed any tears if we lost it. For two pins I'd make Dick throw the thing overboard; there's no sense in taking unnecessary risks. Hang on for a bit; I'll go back and finish my lunch and then relieve you while you have a bite yourself.' Biggles returned to the cabin where he found Ginger and Dick regarding a pile of banana skins with considerable satisfaction. 'Have you finished your lunch, Ginger?' he asked.

'I think I've had my share,' admitted Ginger.

'Then you might go through and relieve Algy for a few minutes while he comes in for his,' Biggles said, as he prepared to resume his interrupted meal.

Ginger disappeared through the doorway, but came back almost immediately. 'Land-ho!' he called.

'Good,' replied Biggles. 'Is Algy coming?'

'He's looking at something ahead; he can't make out what it is, and I think he's getting a bit worried. It looks to me like a storm of some sort. Maybe you'd better go and have a dekko.'

Biggles finished his bread-and-cheese quickly, tore a banana from the reduced bunch, and went back to the cockpit. 'What's the matter?' he asked Algy, who was staring forward through the windscreen.

'What do you make of that?'

Biggles took one long piercing look forward and put the banana in his pocket. 'I don't know, but I don't like the look of it,' he answered shortly. 'We're in the hurricane belt here, don't forget, and when it does decide to blow, things happen. You'd better let me take over. Go and snatch a mouthful of food while you can – and you'd better tell the others to get ready to hang on to something. That's dirty weather coming if I know anything about it.' Biggles slipped into the seat Algy had vacated and fixed his eyes ahead on what was an impressive if rather alarming spectacle.

Some twenty miles away, from out of a motionless sea that resembled nothing so much as a floor of polished steel, rose a large, crescent-shaped island that towered up to a jagged peak in the centre. Beyond it, and on either side, misty blue with distance, were others, their bases merging so softly with the sea that they appeared to float in space. But it was not this impression of dreamlike tranquillity that caused Biggles's lips to come together in a hard line. It was a dark, indigo ridge that was rising with incredible speed above the horizon, almost as if an unseen hand was drawing a giant curtain across the blue dome overhead.

For a moment he hesitated, uncertain whether it would be better to try to get above the storm, or race for the big island in the hope of finding a sheltered anchorage in which to ride it out. Making up his mind to adopt the latter plan, he opened the master throttle to its fullest extent, and thrust the joystick forward for all the speed he could get.

Algy reappeared almost immediately. 'What are you doing?' he asked.

'We're in for a snorter,' muttered Biggles grimly. 'We should use up all our petrol if we ran away from it, or tried to get round it, so I am hoping to reach the island before it hits us. If we can find a cove on the leeward side we ought to be able to weather anything in a craft of this size.'

Algy nodded, satisfied with Biggles's judgement, but a worried frown that deepened quickly to real apprehension settled on his face as he watched the ominous mass sweeping towards them. 'I never saw anything quite like that in my life,' he muttered. 'Looks terrifying, doesn't it?'

'That stuff is travelling at a hundred miles an hour, if it's moving an inch,' replied Biggles tersely. 'We shall go up in the air like a feather if it hits us. Tell the boys to stow everything and lie on the floor.'

'Can we make the island, do you think?'

'I'm hoping so, but it's going to be a close thing.'

They were down to a thousand feet now, roaring over an ocean that was just beginning to stir uneasily, like a sleeping giant who senses danger.

'The water is calm, anyway,' observed Algy optimistically.

'It won't be in a minute,' retorted Biggles grimly. 'The wind that's coming will blow up such a sea as I've no desire to be on. It's going to be touch and go. We—'

'Look out! Mind you don't hit that bird,' interrupted Algy.

Biggles altered his course slightly to keep clear of a great white albatross that came swerving across their bows, outspread wings vibrating, like those of a rook trying to reach a cornfield in the teeth of a gale.

'Look out!' Algy's warning cry rose to a shrill crescendo.

Biggles did not really need the warning. He could see the bird clearly enough. Watching it, he saw it swerve again and come tearing towards them like a piece of tissue paper in a high wind. He did his best to avoid it but it almost seemed as if the bird deliberately charged the aircraft. At the last second Algy flung up an arm to protect his face. Biggles flinched.

There was a splintering crash as the bird struck the machine. Algy, when he had seen that a collision was unavoidable, had ducked below the level of the windscreen. At the crash of the impact he turned a white, startled face upwards. The roar of the engines ceased abruptly.

'It flew slap into the port prop! Smashed it to pieces!' yelled Biggles, wiping a spatter of blood from his face. 'Look!'

Algy got up and saw that only the boss remained on the shaft of the port engine. Of the propeller itself there was no sign, but a nasty red mess of blood and feathers jammed against the splintered windscreen told its own story. 'Good heavens!' he muttered through dry lips, as the starboard engine came to life again when Biggles opened the throttle. 'Can we hold our height on one engine?'

Biggles, who had cut both engines in his anxiety, looked at the island through the fast approaching murk. The sun had disappeared and the black curtain was almost overhead. The sea was glassy. 'We might,' he said simply. 'We can only try.'

As he spoke, a white ruffle shimmered across the water

beneath them, and the flying-boat soared like a ship riding a big roller. 'Here she comes,' he said grimly, and took a fresh grip of the joystick. The island, now white-fringed with breakers, was not more than two miles away.

The ruffle on the sea died away, but Biggles was not deceived. He knew that the lull would not last for more than a few seconds, after which the full force of the hurricane would strike them. 'Hang on,' he said crisply. 'She'll buck like a wild horse when we hit the next lot. Look at the island.'

Algy was already looking at it, and his lips parted with anxiety at what he saw. The jungle with which it was covered was writhing until the whole island seemed to shake like a jelly. Palm fronds and debris whirled high into the air and sped away before the wind like smoke.

Biggles jammed the stick still further forward as he spied a little sheltered cove, protected on the seaward side by a coral reef, now half buried under a smother of foam.

At that moment the hurricane struck them.

The flying-boat rocketed like a wounded pheasant, and half turned over, but Biggles fought it back to even keel, and then put the nose down in a dive that was not far short of vertical. Quivering, twisting, and vibrating like a live thing, the machine crept slowly nearer to the lagoon. The needle of the air-speed indicator rested on the one hundred and forty mark, but the speed at which they approached their objective could not have been more than thirty or forty miles an hour, which meant a wind velocity of a hundred miles an hour. Still, they continued to make way towards the reef, now a swirling, seething, churning line of milk-white foam and spray less than a hundred feet below.

'We shall do it,' shouted Algy exultantly, and at that moment their remaining engine cut out dead.

Apart from a tightening of his jaw muscles, Biggles's expression did not change. He slammed the joystick forward viciously and held it with both hands, his one idea now being to reach dry land regardless of what happened to the machine. He knew only too well that if they were forced down on the water the seas that would follow the wind would swamp them within five minutes. He threw a fleeting glance at Algy. 'Get ready to swim!' he yelled. 'I'm going to try to reach those rocks over there, but I don't think we shall quite manage it. It will have to be every one for himself when she strikes. Tell the boys to get their clothes off and jump for it if we get close enough.'

'But what about the machine?' shouted Algy aghast.

'Let it go hang. If we can save our lives we shall be lucky,' answered Biggles desperately.

Yard by yard the flying-boat crept nearer to the rocks which Biggles had now made his objective, but for every yard it gained it lost three feet of height. It was nearly on the water. Subconsciously, Biggles was aware of the others crowding behind him, throwing off their clothes. The noise of the waves and the scream of the wind in the wires made normal speech futile. 'Get ready!' he roared.

Dick clutched the edge of the cockpit as the machine hovered for an instant on the edge of the rocks.

'The wing!' yelled Biggles. 'The wing! Slide down the wing!'

Dick saw instantly what he meant. The port wing was actually hanging over the rocks. In a flash he was on it, but before he could find a handhold, a terrific gust had caught the machine and whirled it round, so that instead of being over the rocks he was now over the churning water. For one dreadful moment he clawed frantically at the smooth fabric, seeking in vain for a handhold, sliding all the time nearer to the trailing edge. Another gust shook the machine; the wing seemed to drop like a lift under him and he was flung clean into space. For a fleeting instant he seemed to hang in the air, with the foam-capped waves leaping up to meet him, then he was struggling in a deep blue world with unseen monsters that dragged him this way and that, choking the life out of him as they did so. The blue world began to grow darker, with little flecks of white light flashing in it. Dick knew that he was drowning. And just as he knew that whatever else happened he must open his mouth to breathe, the blueness exploded into white daylight. He gave a great gasp. Air poured into his lungs, but before he could see where he was, or even think of swimming, he was down in the blue world again, fighting a hopeless battle against the unseen clutching hands. He knew that he could not fight much longer. His strength was nearly gone. It would be easier not to fight, but to allow the hands to drag him where they would. They were pushing him up again now – up – up – up.

Again he burst into daylight. Again he breathed. Weakly, he looked around for something to which he might cling, but all he could see through a smother of foam was a white line of breakers over which tall, graceful palms were tossing their wind-torn crowns. Feebly he struck out towards them, but before he had taken three strokes he was down in the blue world again, turning over and over as he was borne along, as lightly as a feather, in the heart of a wave. A sound like distant thunder, growing ever louder, reached his ears. It seemed to swell in volume until it was all around him, pulverizing him with sound. Then, just as he thought he could bear it no longer, he struck something solid, and clutched at it wildly. But it seemed to slip between his fingers, ever eluding his frenzied grip. Then miraculously the blue world faded away; the noise abated suddenly, and he found himself kneeling on a bank of sand and shingle that was sliding swiftly back towards the churning waves. In his hands were the rolling stones on which he had striven to obtain a grip. Panting, eyes wide with horror, he saw another white-crested wave rushing towards him, its top,

91

flecked with green, curling ominously. Weakly he struggled to his feet and began fighting his way up the shelving beach.

He knew that the wave would catch him. He could hear it as it hissed along; he could feel it overtaking him, towering high above him. Knowing that he could not escape, he dropped to his knees and dug his hands deeply into the loose stones, at the same time trying to get a grip on them with his feet and knees. He just had time to snatch a last deep breath when the wave, with a roar like an express train, overwhelmed him. In a flash he was whipped up from his unstable handhold and the blue demons had him in their clutches again. Swiftly the blue deepened to indigo, then slowly to black, across which darted flashes of vivid lightning. In his ears was the beating of a thousand drums and the clanging of bells, but the noise grew fainter and fainter as he slipped over an invisible precipice and plunged downwards into a bottomless void.

He seemed to be falling for a long time. It was not an unpleasant sensation, but he wished it would end. He could see the earth now, in the distance, a vague, misty plain coming up to meet him. Down – down – down he plunged, towards a world of silence, leaving the thunder far behind. The earth leapt upwards. As he struck it, it seemed to explode in a great blaze of crimson flame.

Chapter 8

Wrecked

Out of the corner of his eyes Biggles saw Dick go overboard and disappear under the foam, but he could do nothing to help him. Indeed, as he fought to keep the flying-boat under control, it seemed certain that during the next minute or two the others must join him. Ashen, he looked at Algy. 'Jump when she hits!' he cried, in a shrill, strangled voice, and dived deliberately at the rocks.

He did not quite reach them. The machine struck the sea a few yards short, but the result of the impact was almost the same as if she had struck solid earth. There was a rending crash as the wings tore off at the roots, and the bows crumpled like a crushed eggshell.

Ginger jumped. He landed on a rock, but it was wet and slippery with seaweed, and he slid back into the water, only to be thrown up again by the next wave. Algy followed him. He landed short but, providentially, the next wave carried him in so that he could grasp the hand that Ginger, with great presence of mind, held out to him. Gasping, he flung himself flat on the rock and took a grip on the slippery weed.

All this had taken place in a second of time, and before Biggles could get clear of the cockpit the shattered aircraft had been blown a good twenty yards from the land, where it rolled in a boiling maelstrom. To jump now, he saw, would be suicidal, so he threw off his clothes and clung to the top of the hull, ready to make a leap for the shore should an opportunity present itself. But, unhappily, although the force of the storm seemed to have abated suddenly, the wind was still strong enough to blow the aircraft farther and farther from the rock on which the others crouched, and Biggles could only hang on and watch helplessly as the shore receded and the big seas began to batter the flying-boat to pieces.

Algy and Ginger, safe ashore although not a little bruised, clambered along the rocks waiting for the end that now seemed inevitable. It was apparent that the aircraft could not survive the punishment it was receiving for many more minutes; already it was sinking fast. They followed it as far as they could, but presently a great mass of rock, round which the aircraft was drifting, barred their way. Frantically they sought a way over it, but in vain, and the last they saw of him, as the machine was blown beyond the point, Biggles was still clinging to the half-submerged hull. With horror-stricken eyes they watched the machine out of sight beyond the rock.

'Come on! We must do something!' cried Ginger, in a voice shrill with anxiety. He was naked except for a pair of elastic topped trunks. His wet hair was plastered down over his face, while blood from a cut in his shoulder, where it had struck the rock, mingled with the water that poured down his body so that it formed little pink rivulets.

Algy started up, limping, vaguely conscious of a pain in his right ankle; but such was his state of mind that he did not even look to see what had caused it. 'He's being carried out to sea,' he cried in a choking voice. 'We must get to the other side of this rock.'

'We can't get over it; we shall have to find a way round,' muttered Ginger.

'What about Dick?'

'I'm afraid he's gone. We can't do anything about him, anyway. Let's try to see what happens to Biggles.'

They started off in a direction at right angles to the one taken by the flying-boat with the object of forcing a passage through the jungle that overhung the inland side of the rock barring their passage.

'We shall never get through this stuff,' declared Algy in something like a panic.

'We've got to!'

They did their best, but the task, almost naked as they were, was practically impossible. A direct course was out of the question, but by following the most open places in the luxuriant vegetation they were able to make some progress up the side of the fairly steep hill that flanked the mass of rock they were so anxious to get round. Thorns pricked their feet, briers and trailing lianas clutched at their legs and bodies, but they pushed on, hardly feeling the pain.

Ginger was first to reach the top, where he pulled up suddenly, staring out to sea. His face, already pale, turned as white as a sheet. 'Look!' he muttered hoarsely.

Algy, following the direction of his trembling forefinger, said nothing. There was no need to say anything. The end of the tragedy was there before their eyes. Nearly a mile away the hull of the wrecked aeroplane was still wallowing in the waves, but of Biggles there was no sign.

For several minutes, during which neither of them spoke, they stared at the storm-churned water between the wreck and the shore. Then Algy drew a deep breath. 'He's gone,' he said simply.

Ginger bit his lip. 'Yes, he's gone,' he said in a dull voice. Sitting down, he buried his face in his hands.

For two or three minutes they remained thus, Algy staring out across the white-capped waves, loath to abandon hope. 'I'm afraid it's no use standing here,' he said at last, in tones of utter misery. 'Let's go back to see if we can find Dick.'

Slowly they retraced their steps, or rather, they tried to, but it was soon clear to both of them that they had lost their original path. Not that they cared particularly. One way seemed as good as another. They knew that by going downhill sooner or later they would come to the seashore, which they did, striking it at a long, sandy beach. Two things caught their eyes at once. One was an elevator that had been torn off the ill-fated aircraft, and the other, a dark object that was being rocked gently to and fro at the extremity of the surging waves. They hurried towards it.

'It's Dick's jacket,' said Algy unnecessarily, for there was no mistaking the water-soaked garment that he dragged from the edge of the sea. He picked it up and stood staring at it, not knowing what to do with it, yet unwilling to cast it aside. Holding it thus, something fell from a pocket and dropped flat on the white coral sand. It was the doubloon.

Slowly Ginger stooped and picked it up, and gazed at it pensively as it lay in the palm of his hand. 'I think Biggles was about right,' he said heavily. 'One way or another, this piece of metal seems to have caused a good deal of trouble.'

Algy nodded. 'Yes,' he agreed. 'I think I've seen about as much of that coin as I want to.'

'Then the sooner it goes where it can't do any more harm, the better,' declared Ginger viciously, and throwing back his arm, was about to hurl the doubloon far out to sea when he was arrested in the act by the sound of a distant rifle shot.

'What the deuce!' muttered Algy, staring in the direction whence the sound had come, which appeared to be just beyond the end of the strand on which they stood.

'It couldn't be Biggles because he couldn't possibly have got there in the time, and he hadn't a rifle, anyway,' muttered Ginger. 'This island must be inhabited. Perhaps there is a town or a village a little farther along.'

'Maybe it's a trading-station, or something,' murmured Algy vaguely. 'You had better hang on to the doubloon; after all, it's gold, and it may enable us to buy food or clothes. Let's go and have a look.'

They set off at a brisk pace, Algy limping on his injured

ankle, which a swelling suggested had been wrenched. But with the aid of a piece of driftwood, which he used as a walking stick, he was able to make fairly good progress.

It was farther to the end of the beach than they thought; in fact, it must have been a good two miles, for they were more than half an hour reaching it, by which time it was beginning to get dark.

Facing them, at the end of the gently curving bay round which they had walked, a mass of boulders lay like a great wall athwart the beach, high on the landward side, but sloping steeply down into the sea, evidently an old landslide from the hills that towered up in the centre of the island. From it sprang a small but graceful group of coconut palms.

'If we can get to the top of that pile we ought to be able to see who fired the shot, if he's still there,' observed Algy.

With a quickening sense of expectancy they scrambled up over the boulders, and arriving at the crest near the palms, stood rooted to the ground in astonishment at what they saw.

In a small lagoon, made perfect by a coral breakwater that lay across the entrance, rode an aeroplane. One glance was sufficient to reveal that it was the amphibian that had been stolen from them in Marabina. Like a giant sea-bird, it sat lightly on the water, rocking gently in the swell coming in through the opening that gave access to the sea. It was some thirty or forty yards from the shore, on which lay the collapsible canoe that had formed part of its equipment, and about the same distance from another landslide that formed the farther side of the natural harbour.

After one swift, incredulous glance, Algy's eyes had switched to the beach and the jungle behind it, seeking the men he fully expected to see. But to his blank surprise there was no sign of them. He turned to Ginger. 'Well, what do you make of that?' he said tersely.

'Deutch and his crowd must be here.'

'Without any shadow of doubt.'

'Then—' a sudden, almost unbelievable possibility rushed into Ginger's mind '—then this must be *the* island,' he whispered, almost breathlessly.

Algy stared at him. Curiously enough, that possibility had not occurred to him. 'What an amazing chance,' he said.

'What can we do about it?'

'What *can* we do?'

'We can get our machine.'

Algy looked at the sea, still flecked with white, and shook his head. 'How?' he asked. 'There isn't room to take off in the lagoon; she'd be swamped in five seconds in the open sea, and the beach is nothing like big enough for a land take-off. We can't lift the machine over these rocks to the beach on the other side. Besides, it's nearly dark. It seems a pity, but I'm afraid there is nothing we can do about it except hide up and wait for another opportunity. It's something to know the machine is here, anyway.' He spoke without enthusiasm, for the dreadful uncertainty of Biggles's fate – for he still hoped, although in his heart he feared the worst – left him careless of the future. 'Let's get away from here in case Deutch happens to come back. No doubt he is treasure hunting,' he concluded.

By mutual consent, they walked quickly along the ridge on which they stood in order to reach the woods, but if they thought their adventures were over for the day they were soon to be disillusioned. They were among the slim boles of the coconut palms, looking for the easiest way down, when they almost collided with a slight, pale faced man, coming in the opposite direction. He was a stranger to them, but his first words, and the manner in which he instantly covered them with the rifle he carried, left them in no doubt as to his identity.

'Waal, waal,' he drawled. 'Say now, ain't that jest too

dandy. Come right along. Deutch was hopin' you'd drop in sometime!'

Algy eyed the speaker dispassionately. He felt no fear. His only sensation was one of cold anger. 'You're 'Frisco Jack, I suppose?'

'Sure! Come on, let's go, or we may slip on these stones in the dark.'

Algy and Ginger were quite helpless, and they had the sense to realize it. Without speaking, they accompanied their captor to the far side of the lagoon where, in a small open space that had previously been hidden from their sight by an outcrop of rock, three men were seated. Deutch was one; a tall man with a slight cast in his deep set eyes, was another; the third was an enormous black man wearing a uniform so elaborate that in different circumstances he might have cut a comical figure. But there was nothing funny about the way he sprang to his feet when the small party appeared, and stood glowering, his mouth half open with surprise and the fingers of his hands slowly opening and closing.

'So you've got here, hey?' began Deutch, addressing Algy, after the first buzz of astonishment had died away.

'It looks like it, doesn't it?' answered Algy evenly.

'You keep a civil tongue in your head, my cock, or I'll make you sing a different tune,' snarled Deutch. 'Where's your smart partner – the tall feller?'

'I wish I knew,' replied Algy briefly.

'Come on; no lies. Where is he?'

Algy was in no mood for lying. In fact, he was so utterly sick that he didn't care much what happened. 'To the best of my knowledge he was drowned about an hour ago,' he said curtly. 'Our ship was smashed to pieces in the hurricane. It fell into the sea. As far as I know we are the only survivors. Now you know the whole story.'

Silence fell for a moment or two. There was something so

convincing in the way in which Algy had spoken that they could not do other than believe him.

'That comes o' bein' too clever,' sneered Deutch. He turned to the others. 'What shall we do with 'em, boys?'

The black man grinned broadly. In an instant he had whipped out a razor which he began to whet in a horrible manner on the palm of his hand.

'Put that thing away,' growled the cross-eyed man. 'If there's any bumpin' off to be done, let's have it clean. Why not turn 'em loose? They can do no harm.'

'And have 'em slipping off with the machine? These guys can fly, don't forget,' grated the American harshly.

'They might know something about – what we're looking for,' suggested Deutch thoughtfully.

'Sure; so they might,' agreed 'Frisco Jack. 'Why not tie 'em up and ask 'em a few questions in the morning? Maybe they'll feel different then. Anyway, there ain't no sense in doin' nothin' in a hurry.'

'Maybe you're right,' agreed Deutch. 'That's it, tie 'em up. We can allus get rid of 'em when they ain't no more use. Get a bit o' rope, Pedro.'

Pedro found a piece of cord amongst the pile of stores that lay a little to one side, and grabbed Ginger, who was nearest, by the arm. Involuntarily, Ginger's fingers opened under the pressure, and the doubloon, which he was still carrying, fell out of his hand on to the sand.

With a whoop of joy Pedro snatched it up. 'Whar you get this?' he growled, showing it to the others.

Ginger did not reply.

'Where'd you get it?' snapped Deutch.

'It's the original coin we had in London,' replied Ginger, coolly.

'Tha's a lie. Mallichore's got that 'n,' snarled Pedro. 'They know where t'others are.'

'Where did you get it?'

'I tell you it's the same one,' protested Ginger wearily. 'We got it from Mallichore with the rest of our things. Do we look as if we've been treasure hunting?' he concluded sarcastically.

'Pass it over to me, Pedro,' ordered Deutch.

For a moment Pedro hesitated, obviously reluctant to part with the coin, and the thought flashed into Algy's mind that a similar incident had been enacted, not long before, perhaps on that very spot, when Dick's father had refused to give the coin up to Deutch.

'Let me keep it, boss,' pleaded Pedro.

'All right. There'll be plenty more of 'em presently,' agreed Deutch in a surly voice.

With a grin of delight Pedro slipped the doubloon into his pocket; then, taking the cord, he tied Ginger's wrists and ankles and pushed him brutally on to the ground. Fortunately, the sand was soft. He then treated Algy in the same way.

By the time this was done night had fallen, but the moon came up and flooded the lagoon with a silvery radiance.

'Frisco Jack fetched a blanket and spread it out on the sand. The others, including Deutch, did the same. 'We'll attend to you in the morning,' was his parting threat, as he regarded his captives with unpleasant satisfaction.

Chapter 9

What Happened to Dick

Had Algy or Ginger, at the time when they had recovered Dick's jacket from the sea, looked a little more closely to the left, where great heaps of seaweed, torn from the ocean bed by the fury of the hurricane, had been cast up, they might have noticed a little white crumpled heap, half buried under long ribbons of slimy kelp, in which case this story would have had a different ending. For the crumpled heap was Dick's bruised body, pounded into unconsciousness by the weight of the giant rollers which had, at the finish, flung him far up the gently shelving beach.

For a long time after Algy and Ginger had gone the pathetic figure did not move. It might have been a corpse. The sun sank. The tide ebbed. The moon came up, and presently cast a pale, eerie light on Dick's pallid face. A crab marched out of a hole in a rock, a curious crab with high, stilt-like legs, and long waving antennae. With a soft clicking noise it advanced with the characteristic movement of its kind upon the recumbent form. Two yards away it stopped, as if suspecting a trap. Another joined it. Presently came others, until they formed a semicircle on the seaward side of the motionless figure. The quiet of the night was filled with their soft clicking. Slowly the serried ranks advanced.

Slowly, also, the moonbeams moved across Dick's deathlike face until they reached his eyes. He stirred uneasily. Instantly the clicking army receded like a wave.

He moaned weakly. Then, suddenly, he opened his eyes. For a moment or two he stared vacantly at the star-spangled sky. With a rush consciousness returned, and he sat up, resting on his right hand, gazing at the shining sea. For a full minute he remained thus while he strove to separate dreams from reality. Then, knowing the truth at last, he tried to stand up. Instantly he was violently sick, evacuating vast quantities of sea-water. This not only relieved him but restored him to full consciousness, and he managed to get to his feet, stiffly, feeling his bruised body with shaking fingers.

Another spell of nausea passed, and he looked round to see where he was. He did not expect to see the others. Nor did he. Nor could he see any signs of the aircraft. A feeling of terrible loneliness crept over him as he realized that he was alone. It was impossible to believe that the others had all been drowned, but it was equally impossible to believe that they had been saved. A white object lying on the high-water mark some distance away caught his eye, and he walked unsteadily towards it. Before he reached it he saw that it was an elevator, and tears that he could not keep back welled to his eyes as he realized what it portended. Sick with weariness and grief, he sank down on the sand and buried his face in his hands.

A little while later, however, as the spasm of misery expended itself, he got up again and contemplated his own position. Not that he was concerned particularly about it; his distress was far too poignant for that. Nevertheless, he felt an uncomfortable twinge as he regarded the silent jungle that rose up like a towering wall behind him. What terrible beasts did it harbour? What horrors crouched in its sable heart? He did not know, but it was impossible not to feel its hidden menace.

Fighting down his fears by sheer will-power, he turned and looked back at the sea, recognizing at once the scene of the disaster. There were the rocks that he had tried to reach, left high and dry by the receding tide; there, also, was the place where Biggles had tried to crash the flying-boat; the great buttress of rock jutted far out, but the lashing waves were no longer there. Perhaps – the others – were lying there, he thought miserably. What was it his father used to say? The sea always gives up its dead.

Looking to right and left for something he dreaded to find, he began to walk towards the end of the buttress of rock which Algy and Ginger had been unable to surmount; but now, because the tide had ebbed, it was possible to walk right round it. He reached the end and climbed up on the lowest rocks, still looking for what he feared to find – the bodies of his comrades. Satisfied that they were not there, he retraced his steps, and walking up to the dry sand beyond the high-water mark, as near to the forest as he dared go, he sat down to rest and wonder what he should do. Water was his most pressing need; his mouth was parched, but he did not feel like exploring in the moonlight and the grotesque shadows that it cast. So, with his chin cupped in the palm of his right hand, and his eyes fixed unseeingly on the mass of rock, he prepared to wait for dawn.

How far distant it was, he had, of course, no means of knowing, because he had no idea of how long he had been unconscious. Thus he sat for a long time. Never had a night seemed so long. Fortunately the air was warm, or in his nude condition his misery would have been intensified. Slowly the time passed. The moon moved silently on its allotted course; it crept round the bay that lay at his right hand until at last it bathed the rocks on his left in its blue radiance.

He was nearly asleep when he saw one of the rocks move – or thought he saw it move. He had, in fact, sunk into that condition midway between sleep and wakefulness when one hesitates to believe what one sees. But he was wide awake instantly, holding his breath, every nerve taut. Slowly the rock took shape; it became a human figure, and as he stared with wide, affrighted eyes he knew that he was dreaming. Either that, or he was seeing something at which he had always scoffed. A ghost. For the figure was not that of an ordinary man. Around its head was tied a spotted handkerchief, the corners hanging down over the nape of the neck. A vest, woven in a pattern of wide, alternate bars, covered the chest, the lower part ending in crimson, pleated pantaloons, which were tucked into wide-topped boots with silver buckles, on which the moon shone brightly. In its hand it carried an enormous cutlass, the point of which rested on the rock.

With parted lips, his heart palpitating wildly, Dick could only stare, while the figure slowly turned, and raising its hand to shield its eyes, gazed long and steadily down the coral strand. Then, as mysteriously as it had appeared, it had gone.

In Dick's mind there was no longer any doubt. It was the ghost of a long-dead buccaneer. A spirit walking in death the path it had trodden in life. He waited for no more. With a convulsive gasp he sprang to his feet and set off along the sand as fast as his legs could carry him. And not until another pile of rocks appeared ahead did he begin to slow down, looking back fearfully over his shoulder. Seeing nothing of the apparition, however, he paused to recover his breath. Relieved, he set off again, making for a clump of coconut palms that rose up from the rocks, for he recognized them for what they were and hoped to find a fallen nut from which he might be able to quench his thirst.

Reaching his objective, he was casting about on the ground when something just beyond the rocks caught his eye, an object that shone white in the moonlight. For a moment he stared unbelievingly. He rubbed his eyes and stared again. But there was no mistake. The gleam that had caught his eye was the moonlight playing on the white wings of an aeroplane that rode lightly on the still water of a small lagoon. Naturally, it did not occur to him that it was any other than the machine in which he had arrived – or rather, from which he had fallen – and he was half way towards it when he saw his mistake. He pulled up dead, choking back the cry of joy that rose to his lips and struggling to understand the full significance of what he saw. Was he dreaming again, or was it the Sikorsky? It looked like it. Could it be possible, he asked himself? He soon realized that it could, and what its presence meant. But where was the crew – Deutch and the others? If the aircraft was here, it meant that they were here, too. They could not be far away. Standing quite still, he surveyed the shore of the lagoon, foot by foot, yard by yard. But still he could not see them. He had just made up his mind to approach nearer when he heard a sound that sent the blood racing through his veins. It was unmistakable. Someone, not far away, had snored.

He moistened his lips, wondering how to take advantage of the situation. There was the machine, but he could not fly it. He did not even know how to start the engines. But there, lying on its side on the beach, was the canoe, and that was something he did understand. But of what use was that to him? At that moment he could not see how it could help him, unless he took it right away and hid it, when at some future date it might enable him to reach another island or the mainland. Yes, he decided, that was what he would do. He would take the canoe. But first of all he would try to find out what Deutch and the others were doing. Raising his eyes, he saw that the sky was paling and knew that the dawn could not be far off. Soon it would be light, so whatever he proposed doing would have to be done quickly.

Swiftly, but making no sound and keeping well in the

dense black shade of the jungle, he crept towards the place from which the snore had come. Again he heard the sound, and although it made his skin turn to gooseflesh, he kept on. With his heart seeming to beat in his throat, but making no more noise than a shadow, he crept nearer to the rocks, and at last peeped over them. He was down again instantly. Six figures were lying on the sand, four dressed and two undressed. Why six? The Americans had said that there were only four people on board the machine when it was stolen. He risked another peep, a longer one this time. As he did so, one of the nearest figures, one of the undressed ones, moaned slightly and turned towards him. Instinctively his eyes went to his face, and he recognized Algy.

The shock of this discovery was so terrific that he was only just able to stifle a cry. As it was, it left him weak and trembling. Hardly able to breathe, he looked again, and saw, as he already half suspected, that the other undressed figure was Ginger. He also saw from their positions that their hands and wrists were tied.

He almost panicked as he realized his helplessness to assist them. Never in his life had he wanted anything so much as he wanted a knife at that moment. Could he untie the knots? He could not do less than try, he decided. He glanced again at the sky, and groaned inwardly as he saw that the once-longed-for dawn was now approaching all too quickly. At any moment the others might awake. It was now or never.

Steeling himself, he crept swiftly round the rocks and approached Algy, who was the nearer. He saw that his eyes were wide open and saw the look of wonderment that leapt into them, but he did not stop. In a moment he was down beside him, working at his fettered ankles. His heart sank as he saw how tightly the knots were drawn, and realized that it would take some time to undo them.

He started as Algy struggled into a sitting position, but

then saw that he was trying to tell him something. 'The razor,' he breathed.

Dick, following the direction of his eyes, saw what he meant. A few yards away a large black man in a blue coat lay stretched out on the sand; beside him, half open, lay a razor. With a little gasp of relief, he moved towards it. His hand went out, fingers outspread. At that moment the man awoke.

For one ghastly moment they stared into each other's eyes. Then, with an oath, the man sprang to his feet.

'Run for it, Dick.' It was Algy's voice, clear and sharp.

It galvanized Dick into violent activity. In a sort of dreadful nightmare, he leapt aside just as the man snatched up the razor and aimed such a slash at him that had the weapon reached its mark it would have taken his head from his shoulders. With an involuntary cry of horror, he darted up the rocks with the alacrity of a mountain goat, and then, taking the far side in a dozen bounds, he set off up the beach as if a pack of demons was at his heels. In the grip of stark panic, he dared not risk a glance behind until he had covered a good hundred yards; when he did, his worst fears were realized. The man was leaping down the rocks in hot pursuit, something in his hand reflecting brightly the rays of the sun, the rim of which was now showing above the horizon.

A shot rang out. Sand spurted from under Dick's feet and urged him to even more frenzied efforts, but he had the good sense to swerve, which may have been as well, for another bullet, with a vicious *zip*, tore a long furrow in the sand. On he raced, his feet flying over the pounded coral, and not until he was within striking distance of the rocky *massif* on which he had seen the ghost of the buccaneer did he snatch another fleeting glance over his shoulder. For a moment his knees seemed to sag as he saw that the other man was not only racing along in his footsteps but had halved the distance between them. Seeing that he could not climb the rock that lay across his path, he swerved wildly towards the seaward end round which the incoming tide was now flowing. He nearly fell under his own impetus as the water dragged at his shins, but with an effort he recovered his balance and rounded the point. In front of him lay another stretch of beach, terminating in more rocks, and, slightly out to sea, a rocky islet.

Again he set off at full pelt, glancing often at the tangle of jungle on his left hand in case an avenue of escape should offer itself in that direction. But it appeared to be impenetrable, and he dare not risk a halt to explore in case that should, in fact, prove to be the case.

His strength was nearly gone and he was catching his breath in great gasps by the time he reached the next barrier of rocks. He knew that he could not run much farther. As it was, only the dreadful fear inspired by the heavy footsteps behind him kept him going. Actually, he was running over the same ground that his father had run a few months previously, when he had fled from Deutch, but, of course, he did not know that. He chose the same way up the rocks, and then, at the top, faltered, appalled by what he saw. Before him, as far as he could see, lay a wilderness of broken rock; on the right a headland jutted out towards the islet, but between him and it lay a jungle-filled ravine, through which, naked as he was, he could not hope to force a way. Yet he knew that barefoot on the sharp rocks the man would soon overtake him. With eyes round with despair, he looked for a hiding-place. There were several holes in the rock, some large, some small, and choosing one of them near the edge of the ravine, he jumped into it and lay flat on the bottom.

Motionless, with his hand over his mouth in an attempt to quiet his gasping breath, he heard the man arrive on the rocks, run forward a few paces, and then stop, obviously at a loss to know what had become of him. Then he heard him move forward again. To his unspeakable horror, the footsteps approached his hiding-place. Again they stopped. He breathed again as they began to recede. But it was only for a moment. Slowly, with frequent halts, they came nearer again, and Dick knew that the man, the cut-throat the American had called Pedro, was examining the holes one by one.

Dick knew that if he persisted in this, discovery was inevitable, for the hole in which he lay was not more than five or six feet deep; yet his only chance now was to remain in it.

Slowly, but with dreadful deliberation, the padding steps came nearer. He could hear the heavy breathing of the searcher now. Nearer and nearer they came. Then, very close, they stopped, and in the dreadful silence his heart seemed to stop beating and he had to bite his lip to prevent himself from crying out. At last came the sound he dreaded to hear: a low, horrible chuckle. With a convulsive start he looked up. The man was standing on the lip of his hiding-place, grinning broadly as he whetted his razor on the palm of his hand. Then, dropping flat, he reached downward, and his fingers closed in Dick's hair.

A scream of stark terror that he could no longer repress broke from Dick's lips as he was hauled out, squirming, like a fish from a pool. The man took him in his left hand while his right swept back for the blow.

Instinctively, Dick threw up his arm to protect his throat. He closed his eyes, and kept them shut while an eternity seemed to pass. Then came a crashing report in his ears and he felt himself fall.

At that moment he thought that he was dead. He thought that the fatal blow had been struck. Curiously, he opened his eyes, and was surprised to find that he could still see. No startling alteration had taken place in the scene. The man was still standing there, although the expression on his face had changed. He was no longer smiling. The horrible grin had given way to an expression of comical surprise, and he swayed slowly to and fro like a big tree in a wind. A black hand jerked open and the razor fell, tinkling musically on the hard rock. The hand came up, groping at the breast of the blue coat. For three or four seconds Pedro stood thus; then his legs collapsed suddenly and he pitched forward on to his face.

Instantly, it seemed, his place was taken by another figure, a figure that confirmed Dick's conviction that he was no longer in the world of the living. It was the buccaneer, the ends of his red bandana flapping in the breeze. In his left hand he still carried the cutlass; in his right was a smoking pistol.

Dick stared at the face, speechless, his reeling brain trying to fit together the confusing pieces of a dreamlike jigsaw puzzle. 'Biggles!' he cried weakly.

Chapter 10

What Happened to Biggles

When Biggles, on the sinking aircraft, had been driven beyond the point of rock that hid him from the others' gaze, his position was not quite so desperate as it undoubtedly appeared to them. In the first place, the half empty tanks, and the air filled wings that still trailed behind the hull, gave it a certain degree of buoyancy. Secondly – and this, of course, they could not see – the wreck was being driven towards a small islet, little more than a big mound of rock, that rose out of the water some distance farther along, perhaps two hundred yards from the main island. It appeared to be a piece broken off the end of the island, the very tip of the crescent which in shape it resembled. Beyond it lay the open sea.

Biggles, watching with a degree of anxiety that can be better imagined than described, saw at once that if the wreck went ashore at the islet he might be able to climb up the face of the rock beyond the reach of the waves, from where, when the sea calmed down, he could swim to the island. On the other hand, if it was blown beyond the point, it would certainly be carried out to sea where it would quickly founder.

It was a close thing. At one time he thought he would strike the islet fairly in the centre, but at the last moment a contrary current, or a back-blast of wind, slewed the wreck sideways, so that it became obvious that it would miss it. Observing this, he took a desperate risk, although it was his only possible chance of salvation. He waited for a momentary lull between the waves, and then jumped. He fell short, as he knew he would, but half a dozen desperate strokes took him to an out-jutting crag, to which he clung with the strength of despair. The next wave struck him before he could pull himself up, but he was prepared for it, and although what little breath he had left was beaten out of him by the force of the blow, and the backwash nearly tore his arms out of his body, he managed to drag himself above the water line, where, still drenched by spray, he sank down, utterly exhausted.

For some minutes he remained still, his face buried in his hands, elbows on his knees, while he recovered his strength; then, seeing that he was on the seaward side of the rock, he started climbing to the top, from where he hoped to obtain a view of the island and thus let Algy and Ginger know that he was at least temporarily safe.

Before he reached the actual peak, however, a surprise was in store for him. With a mild shock he realized that the stones over which he was climbing were artificial; that they were hand-hewn in great blocks, forming a sort of ramp, or bastion. It took him some time to find a way over them, but when he did, he saw to his astonishment that he stood in what, in the remote past, had been a fort. A low, castellated wall circumscribed the top of the knoll, which had been levelled and paved with flat stones. Placed at intervals, some pointing landward and some seaward, were six old-fashioned iron cannon on rotting wooden carriages. Small heaps of cannon-balls lay beside them.

Biggles stared about him blankly, realizing that he was standing in one of the many forts that had been established by the navigators and settlers in the great days of discovery.* At one corner a flight of stone steps led downward

* Such forts, with their old cannon still in place, still exist on many of the West Indian islands, and on the Main itself. WEJ

into the heart of the living rock, but with Dick's fate weighing heavily upon him, he was in no mood for exploration. Remembering the others, and the anxiety he knew they must be suffering, he walked over to the landward side, and leaning over the battlements, looked long and steadily at the island, hoping to see them. They were not in sight, however, so as the sea was still in such a state that it would have been suicidal to attempt to swim the channel, he sat down to await their arrival.

For once he was utterly sick at heart. Dick's fate, which he did not for one moment doubt, depressed him to the point of complete dejection. He had grown fond of the lad with his ever-ready cockney wit. The other things, bad as they were, did not really matter. The expedition had gone to pieces. They had lost two machines and all their belongings. They were stranded on an unknown island, without food, without clothes, without weapons – in fact, without anything. Never in all their adventures had they been in such a plight. Meanwhile, Deutch and his companions were no doubt on Treasure Island, using their machine, living on their stores, and perhaps unearthing the doubloons. The memory of the way he had been tricked made him writhe.

In this melancholy mood he could only sit and wait. Where were the others? Why didn't they come? Already the sun was far down; soon it would be dark. The sea was abating rapidly, but it would still be some time before he dare risk the swim. Pensively, he gazed at the rocks nearest to the islet, those on which he would have to land – the 'Land's End' of the island, now softly purple in the glow of the setting sun. Where were Algy and Ginger? Doubts began to assail him. Could it be possible that they had been washed back into the sea after all? Miserable, he could only stand and stare. If he could get to the island he might be able to do something. Looking down, he saw that the face of the rock below him was almost sheer, so he began to walk round the ramparts looking for the easiest way down when the time should come for him to go.

He was not greatly surprised when, on the side opposite to the one up which he had climbed, he saw a number of rough steps cut in the rock, evidently the path used by the builders, and afterwards by the garrison, when a ship called with stores. It struck him suddenly that there ought to be some sort of reservoir in or under the rock, possibly a tank for the collection of rain-water; otherwise the garrison could not have survived a siege; so, as the salt water had parched his mouth, he turned towards the flight of steps that went down apparently into the very heart of the islet. The passage was pitch dark, and it was with a feeling of expectant curiosity that he groped his way downward.

Before he reached the bottom he could see that light was coming in from somewhere, and presently he saw that it entered through cunningly cut apertures in the rock, which admitted just enough twilight for him to make out the details of the chamber in which he shortly found himself. A strange sensation that he was living in the past swept over him as he gazed around.

The interior of the fort was one large room some forty feet square, cut out of the living rock. It gave the appearance of having been hurriedly evacuated. A pile of old clothes lay in one corner, while others were thrown carelessly over an old brass swivel-gun that leaned against a loophole. Propped against the rear wall, curled up in positions which suggested a violent death, were two skeletons. Near the bony fingers of one lay a cutlass, pitted with the rust of centuries, while scattered about the floor were several flintlock muskets and pistols. The only other articles of note were six large barrels. Investigation showed that four of them had

115

probably contained food, either salt pork or *boucan*, for some mouldering bones still remained in three of them, while the fourth was still half full of musty flour. The last two had been used for gunpowder, a little of which remained. In a corner, under a thick coating of dust, was a little pile of objects that looked like marbles. Biggles picked up a handful, but dropped them again at once; he knew by their weight that they were either musket balls, or grape-shot for the swivel gun. There was no sign of a water cistern.

For a little while he stood silent in the gathering gloom obsessed by a morbid depression as he pondered over the frailty of humanity. Who were these men who had left their bones so far from home? What grim tragedy had been enacted here? He could never know. No one would ever know. With a sigh he turned his back on the dismal scene, preferring to wait in the fresh air above, but at the foot of the steps a thought occurred to him, and he strode back to the pile of clothes. He might as well go clad, he thought, if only as a protection against the briers and the mosquitoes which he suspected would soon appear.

He selected three garments: a shirt woven in a pattern of broad horizontal bands, a pair of reddish-coloured breeches, and a spotted handkerchief to tie about his head. They smelt stale, musty, but he did not mind that, for the morrow's sun would, he knew, purify them. Hunting about, he found a pair of old boots that fitted him, also a piece of tarpaulin, and this he took in order to keep the other things dry during his proposed swim to the island. At the last minute, with a curious smile playing about his mouth, he added a brace of pistols, some bullets and a flask of powder. The flask, once soft leather, was as hard as iron, but it still served its purpose. Satisfied that there was nothing more worth taking, he put the things he had selected on the tarpaulin, tied the ends together, and thrusting the cutlass under the knots as a means of carrying the bundle more easily, he returned to the battlements.

He saw at once that the sea had gone down as swiftly as it had got up, and, moreover, the tide had ebbed considerably, lessening the distance of the swim; so, throwing his leg over the low wall, he made his way down the outside steps to the water. Another minute and he had slid gently into it. Then, by swimming on his back and holding his burden clear of the water, he was able to reach the rocks opposite without the contents getting wet.

Finding a convenient place, he shook as much water off himself as possible, after which he donned the old-fashioned garments. This done, he looked about him. The moon had risen; and everything was very still. What dangers lurked, if any? He did not know, but having brought the pistols, he thought he might as well load them, so this he did, and leaving the hammers down for safety, he stuck them in the top of his pantaloons as the easiest way of carrying them. Then, cutlass in hand, he set off along the beach towards the spot where Dick had fallen, and where he had last seen Algy and Ginger on the weed-covered rocks. It still struck him as extraordinary that they had not appeared.

Reaching the spot, he searched the foreshore carefully, but all he found was Dick's jacket, which was lying where Ginger had dropped it when he had heard the distant shot. Slowly he walked on, still searching, dreading to find what he sought, until further progress was interrupted by another barrier of rock. He looked at it for some minutes, and then, deciding that there was no point in going on, he returned to the place where he had landed on the island. On the high-water mark he found some coconuts that had been brought down by the recent hurricane. These he collected, and breaking them with his cutlass, drank the milk with relish. Then, utterly worn out by the day's fatigues, he lay down to rest until the morning.

For a long time he could not sleep. The fate of the others haunted him, but at last, towards dawn, he must have dropped off, for it was broad daylight when a piercing scream of fear brought him staggering to his feet. For a second or two he stood blinking, fighting for complete consciousness, wondering where he was, and if the scream had been part of the nightmare that had disturbed his rest. But then he saw a movement, and knew that it was no dream. Fifty yards away an enormous black man was kneeling, reaching down for something he could not see. Wonderingly, he began to walk towards him, watching with interest as he got to his feet, dragging something up with him. Unbelievingly, he saw that it was Dick. The whole thing was fantastic, but too vivid to be anything but reality. He saw the man's arm go up, and caught the flash of steel. Whipping out a pistol, he dashed forward. At ten yards, seeing that he would be too late if he did not act, he took swift aim and fired. The pistol roared. The man twitched convulsively. Dick slumped to the ground. A razor tinkled on the rock.

Biggles ran forward again just as the man pitched headlong.

Chapter 11

The Rescue

Biggles stooped, caught Dick by the arm and helped him to his feet. 'You're all right now, laddie,' he said kindly. 'I was just about in time, wasn't I?' he added gravely.

Dick nodded. He was too far gone to speak. The sky seemed to be turning purple. His strength seemed to be running out of his feet.

'Here! Hold up!' cried Biggles sharply. 'We don't allow fainting.'

Dick forced a sickly grin. 'Sorry,' he said, wiping beads of perspiration from his forehead with the back of his hand. 'I thought I was a goner that time.'

'Yes,' agreed Biggles. 'It was touch and go.' As he spoke his eyes focused suddenly on a point just beyond where they were standing. 'Take a look at that,' he said in a low voice, indicating something that lay on the ground. 'It should give you something to think about.'

Dick's eyes followed the point of the rusty blade. He saw Pedro, lying face downwards. On the water-worn rock a few inches from his outflung right hand was a little yellow disk. It was the doubloon.

'As I have remarked before, that coin doesn't seem to bring its owner much luck, does it?' remarked Biggles suspiciously. 'Don't touch it,' he went on sharply, as Dick moved towards it with the obvious intention of picking it up.

'Are you going to leave it lying there?'

Biggles shook his head, the corners of his mouth turned

down. 'I think the sooner it's out of sight the better,' he said grimly. 'I've seen enough of the confounded thing, anyway,' he added almost viciously, as he walked over to the coin. Then abruptly, with the sole of his boot, he kicked it sideways into the hole in which Dick had sought refuge. 'That's that,' he muttered, as it disappeared from sight. 'Now then, my lad, we've got a lot to talk about. I don't mind telling you that you're the last person I expected to meet here. Have you seen anything of Algy or Ginger?'

'I jolly well have!' declared Dick emphatically. 'I was trying to get them away when this devil woke up and chased me.'

'Get them away? Then they're alive! Thank God for that.' Biggles's fervent tone of voice revealed the depth of his relief.

'They're prisoners,' explained Dick quickly.

Biggles stared. 'Prisoners!' he ejaculated.

Briefly Dick described his adventures which had led to the present situation.

When he had finished Biggles drew a deep breath. 'We must get them out of the clutches of these thugs right away,' he declared.

Dick glanced at the figure lying on the ground. 'What about – him?' he asked.

'I can't stop to attend to him now,' answered Biggles coldly. 'His pals will have to do that.' As he spoke, Biggles reloaded the pistol he had fired. 'Bring that razor along,' he ordered. 'If Algy and Ginger are still tied up it will be useful.'

'Where the dickens did you get these things you're wearing?' asked Dick curiously. 'Great Scott! It must have been you I saw last night,' he went on quickly, remembering his moonlight adventure. 'I took you for the ghost of a buccaneer.'

'They were in an old fort I found over there on that islet,' replied Biggles. 'I haven't time to tell you all about it now. I'm worried about the others. Come on, let's march.'

'Are you going to attack the whole gang?' inquired Dick as they walked along the beach in the direction of the lagoon.

'I don't know. We'll spy out the land first, and make our plans afterwards,' replied Biggles. 'I wouldn't hesitate to attack except for one thing, and that's this fellow the American told us about, 'Frisco Jack. Apparently he's by way of being an expert with a revolver, so it would be asking for trouble to get within range of his guns. These pistols I've got are better than nothing, but I wouldn't bet on their accuracy outside a dozen yards. Anyway, I should be sorry to take on 'Frisco Jack with a revolver — Hark! What's that?' He broke off sharply as a loud hail rang out not far away. It appeared to come from the far side of the first barrier of rocks over which they were about to climb, so he crept quietly to the top and peeped over. He was down again in an instant, and grabbed Dick by the arm. 'Quick!' he whispered. 'Into the bushes.'

Dick followed him to the edge of the jungle, and by keeping close behind as he forced a passage, was able to follow without scratching himself very badly. 'Who is it?' he breathed.

''Frisco Jack, I suspect, and he's coming this way. He's probably looking for his friend, or else he's wondering who fired the shot. Not a word; this may be a bit of luck for us.'

From their place of concealment they were able to watch the ex-gangster's movements. He appeared on the top of the barrier, and from this point of vantage gazed along the shore. 'Hi! Pedro!' he hailed. Then, suddenly, he saw the man lying on the rocks where he had fallen, and with a terse oath ran towards him.

'Come on, this is our chance,' breathed Biggles, and began to force a passage to the beach, making for the far side of the rocks, a position in which the American would not be able to see them. Thrusting the bushes aside with as little noise as possible, they soon reached their objective.

'Now then, where is the place you last saw Algy and Ginger?' asked Biggles crisply.

Dick pointed to the next barrier of rocks, the landslide on which grew the clump of coconut palms. 'Just over the other side of that,' he answered.

'Then let's run for it, and try to get there before 'Frisco Jack comes back,' announced Biggles, and suiting the action to the word, he set off at a steady run, glancing round occasionally to see if 'Frisco Jack had reappeared.

To his intense satisfaction there was still no sign of him when they slowed down near the landslide. 'Now then, Dick,' he said quietly. 'This is where you will have to show your mettle. If we don't rescue Algy and Ginger now we may never get another chance. It's no time for half-measures. We shall have to go the whole hog. I don't go about the world shooting at people for the sake of stirring up strife, but, by thunder, when other people start the row I do my best to make things hot for them. We haven't more than two people to tackle, Deutch and the fellow who stole our ship – what's his name? – Harvey. When I stick 'em up at the point of the pistol, you run down and cut the others free. Keep your head down, because if they start any rough stuff I shall let fly. With luck, we ought to be able to rescue Algy and Ginger and get our machine back at the same time. Anyway, that's what I'm aiming to do. But whatever happens, once we've shown ourselves, you must get on with your job, which is to get the others free. Is that clear?'

'Absolutely.'

'Good! Then let's get at 'em.'

With pistol in one hand and cutlass in the other, Biggles ran quickly to the top of the rock. Dick, the razor open and gripped firmly, followed. From the ridge they looked down into the lagoon, and although they could see the aircraft, now close to the gap that led to the open sea, and the canoe lying on the sand, there was no sign of the men they sought.

'They're behind the rocks, over there,' said Dick tensely, pointing with the razor. 'That's where they've made their camp.'

Their feet making no noise on the soft sand, they crept forward and peeped round the outcrop of rock that hid the enemy camp from view. Not more than six paces away sat Deutch, cross-legged, eating something out of a tin. Ginger and Algy were still lying on the ground. Harvey was not there.

Biggles levelled his pistol. 'Hands up, Mr Deutch – and keep them up,' he ordered harshly. 'Any argument from you and I'll blow you in halves. And if you have any doubt about that, just try it,' he added vindictively. 'Go ahead, Dick.'

The expression on Deutch's face was almost comical in its astonishment, but he dropped the tin and raised his hands. Biggles walked over to him and clapped the muzzle of the pistol to his head. 'Keep quite still, please,' he murmured as his eyes darted this way and that, seeking the other man he expected to find. Satisfied that he was not there, he looked towards the spot where Dick was helping the others. Ginger was trying to get on his feet. Algy, his face twisted with pain, was massaging his ankles.

Biggles's lips set in a hard line as he realized what had happened, that the tightness of the cords had temporarily crippled them. 'Dick!' he called. 'Come here.'

Dick ran to him as an obedient dog answers its master.

'Take hold of the handle of this pistol,' ordered Biggles. 'If you feel the muzzle move, don't speak – just pull the trigger.' He relinquished the weapon and went swiftly through Deutch's pockets. Among other things he found a revolver, which he transferred to his left hand, and the maps that had been taken from them at Marabina. He did not particularly want them, but he kept them. This done, he went quickly to Algy and Ginger. One glance, and he saw that it would be some minutes before they would be in a fit state to travel, for their wrists and ankles were badly swollen. 'All right,' he said quietly, 'take your time. Keep rubbing them. Let me know when you think you can hobble as far as the canoe.'

'You're going to take the machine, then, are you?' asked Algy quickly, as he understood what Biggles meant.

'You bet your life I am,' returned Biggles promptly. 'I — what the—'

He spun round as a musical whirr reached his ears. He knew instantly what it was. Someone was operating the self-starter in the amphibian, but before he could do anything – indeed, almost before he was able to move – the engines had sprung to life and the machine was taxi-ing through the breach in the coral reef out on to the open sea. He dashed forward, although he knew it was useless from the start. Before he had taken a dozen steps the amphibian was racing over the water, leaving a creamy trail to mark its passage. With bitter chagrin on his face he returned to the others. 'It must be Harvey,' he said angrily. 'I expected to find him here, and I looked for him, but for some reason or other I did not think of the machine. Well, there he goes; he's one less to contend with, anyway.'

Deutch's face registered vicious satisfaction as the amphibian soared skyward.

Biggles's eyes narrowed. 'I think perhaps a little of your own medicine wouldn't do you any harm,' he murmured vindictively. 'Ginger, just knot those pieces of cord together and truss him up.'

Ginger smiled as he moved forward to obey. 'OK,' he said cheerfully.

'Dick,' went on Biggles, 'go and take a look over the rock to see if 'Frisco is on his way back yet. Give the pistol to Algy; he can take care of Deutch for a minute or two.'

Dick handed over his charge and ran lightly to the top of the rock. One glance, and he was on his way back, gesticulating urgently. 'Buck up! He's coming!' he cried.

Biggles started. 'How far away is he?'

'Not more than a hundred yards, but he's coming very slowly because he's helping Pedro along.'

Biggles thought swiftly. 'Stand by, everybody,' he ordered crisply. 'We shall have to be going.'

Algy raised his eyebrows. 'Are you going to run away from that cheap American crook?' he snorted angrily.

'I am,' replied Biggles curtly. 'I don't believe in taking unnecessary risks. He may be a cheap crook, but he's also a sharp-shooter. If it comes to a shooting match, sooner or later someone will get in the way of a bullet, and it is more likely to be one of us than him. I'd sooner leave him running loose than one of us should get plugged in a place like this where there's no chance of getting medical attention. Let's get out of his way; there will be plenty of time for sniping before we're off this island, if I know anything about it. Come on, jump to it.'

Algy looked at the mass of rock that cut off their retreat on one side, and the thick jungle behind them. 'Which way are you going?' he questioned.

'That way!' Biggles pointed to the sea. 'Dick – Ginger, get down to the canoe and put her on the water. Algy, give me a hand with some of this stuff. We may as well take as much of our own property with us as we can.' He hurried to the pile of stores which their enemies had taken out of the amphibian and began making a heap of those things which he thought would be of most benefit, chiefly tinned foodstuffs.

Algy helped him to carry the stores down to the boat,

which without further delay was pushed off into deep water. Heavily loaded, the rather flimsy craft had only an inch or two of freeboard, but as the sea was flat calm there was little danger of her swamping.

'You guys think you're pretty smart, but I haven't finished with you yet, not by a long shot,' shouted Deutch furiously. 'You wait!'

'We'll be waiting,' promised Biggles as he picked up the paddle and sent the little craft skimming towards the open sea.

'Hey, 'Frisco!' roared Deutch. 'Help! Quick!'

There was an answering shout from the other side of the rock.

'Keep steady if 'Frisco opens fire, or we may capsize,' ordered Biggles tersely as he put his weight behind the paddle.

The boat was about a hundred and fifty yards from the shore when 'Frisco Jack dashed round the corner.

'He's seen us,' said Algy quietly. 'He's got his gun in his hand, and he's running out on to the rocks to get as near to us as he can.'

'I don't think he'll hit us at this distance,' replied Biggles calmly, as he continued to drive the boat through the water. 'Outside a hundred yards revolver shooting becomes pure chance.'

A moment later 'Frisco's automatic crashed, but the bullet that ricochetted off the water was several feet away.

Biggles continued to paddle. 'Take a shot at him, Algy; it will upset his shooting,' ordered Biggles, knowing from experience that it is much more difficult for a marksman to take careful aim when he himself is under fire than when he knows he is secure.

The pistol roared, and they heard the shrill scream of the bullet as it glanced off a rock.

'Frisco continued to fire, but the range was getting longer

every second, and presently he gave it up, and returned to the beach where Deutch was yelling to be released.

Biggles turned the nose of the canoe to the left and took up a new course, keeping parallel with the shore.

'Where are you making for?' asked Algy.

'Can you see an islet just off the end of the island, about half a mile or so ahead?'

'Yes.'

'I think that's the best place for us. We can watch the shore from there, so there will be no risk of a surprise attack while we do two things that are getting overdue. The first is eat, and the other is talk. It's time we had a council of war and reviewed the position, as they say in books.'

'The thing that intrigues me most is, where the deuce you got that amazing clobber you're wearing,' said Ginger curiously.

'I'll tell you about that presently,' answered Biggles, pausing to wipe the perspiration from his forehead, for the sun was now getting very hot. 'Couldn't you fellows find any place to land without barging into Deutch and his crowd?' he inquired caustically.

'You can bet we didn't join him from choice,' replied Algy sarcastically.

Biggles resumed his task and nothing more was said until they reached their objective. He did not land immediately, as Deutch and 'Frisco Jack were standing out on the rocks watching them; instead he passed straight on until the islet was between them and the lagoon, thus concealing their movements. Then, still keeping out of sight, he backed the canoe slowly to the foot of the steps that gave access to the fort. 'Up you go,' he said, looking for something to which to make the painter fast. 'Take the grub with you.'

'Why, what are *you* going to do?' asked Algy.

'I'm just going to slip across to the island for a few coconuts,' returned Biggles. 'I don't know about you, but I

127

could do with a drink. I'll join you in a minute.' As he spoke, he pushed the now lightened canoe clear, and sent it skimming towards the island.

Chapter 12

A Lucky Fall

When he came back, and, after making the canoe secure, climbed up to the fort, he found the others still marvelling at it. They were agog with enthusiasm and excitement, pardonable in the circumstances, for it was impossible for anyone with imagination to be in such a place without feeling something of its romantic, if tragic, associations.

'How on earth did you come to discover it?' asked Ginger.

'To tell the truth, I didn't exactly discover it,' admitted Biggles. 'It was shoved under my nose, so to speak. In other words, this is where I managed to get ashore. Naturally, I climbed to the top to see if I could see anything of you on the island, and this is what I found.'

'But where did you get those clothes?' asked Algy, for the others had not yet been below.

'Downstairs.'

'Are there any more?'

'Quite a lot – of sorts.'

There was a rush for the stairway while Biggles remained on the roof in order to watch the distant lagoon. From where he stood it was just possible to see it, which he realized at once was a great advantage, since it enabled them to keep an eye on their enemies without going ashore. At that moment Deutch and 'Frisco Jack were bending over a dark object on the ground; he thought it was Pedro, and he was still watching them when a cry from below sent him hurrying down.

'Did you know this was here?' asked Algy, pointing to another flight of stairs, leading downwards, which had been exposed by the removal of a stone slab in the centre of which was an iron ring.

'No, I'm dashed if I did,' admitted Biggles. 'I looked for it, too. I suppose I didn't see it because it was buried under those rags.' He pointed to the old clothes that had been turned over and now lay scattered about the floor.

'You looked for it? You mean, you suspected it was there?'

'I thought it was bound to be somewhere.'

'What do you think it is?'

'A water tank, to store the rain water that falls on the roof. How could anyone live here without water? No doubt there is water somewhere on the island, but that wouldn't be much good to a beleaguered garrison. If you go upstairs you can see the hole which drains the roof; the water must run straight through a duct into here. Is there any water in it now, I wonder?'

Biggles picked up one of the bullets from the heap on the floor and tossed it through the yawning hole. A soft splash told him what he wanted to know. 'Draw some up and let's have a look at it,' he said. 'There's the bucket.' He pointed to a black, cylindrical object that lay among the old clothes. Like the powder-flask, it had once been leather, but now, having perished, it was as hard as wood.

Algy picked it up, went down the steps till he reached the water, dipped the utensil in, and returned with it squirting water through several cracks.

Biggles took some up in the palm of his hand and tested it with his lips. 'Seems to be all right,' he said, 'but I'd rather not use it unless I was compelled. I prefer fresh coconut milk. Put the lid back on or someone might tumble in. And let's have a bite to eat; I'm hungry.' Turning away from the reservoir, he smiled broadly as, for the first time, he took in the details of the garments the others had selected. In turning over the old clothes they had all found something to suit themselves.

Algy wore a moth-eaten red shirt with a pair of what had once been white breeches that fitted tightly at the knees. On his head was a chimney-pot hat of the sort commonly worn by sailors during the sixteenth and seventeenth centuries. Ginger had selected a blue and white banded shirt like his own; there was a small hole, with a dark, sinister stain round it, in the breast. Dirty calico trousers covered his lower half. For headgear he had chosen a black, three-cornered hat. Dick, for whom everything had been too large, wore a faded blue silk shirt, which he had tied in round the waist with an old belt, so that the lower part formed a sort of kilt, or skirt. Through the belt he had thrust a large pistol. On his head, pulled down well over his ears, was a crimson night-cap with a tassel on the end.

Biggles looked at him in mock terror. 'By thunder! Israel Hands himself!' he gasped. 'All we need is a Jolly Roger to fly at the peak and we should look as bonny a bunch of pirates as ever boarded a prize or sacked a town.'

The others laughed.

'Israel Hands was one of the pirates in Stevenson's story *Treasure Island*, wasn't he?' asked Ginger. 'I read it once, but that was a long time ago.'

'Stevenson only borrowed the name for his book,' Biggles informed him. 'The original Israel Hands was quarter-master to that shocking ruffian Captain Edward Teach, more often known as Blackbeard, perhaps the most blood-thirsty villain of the whole cut-throat crowd, excepting possibly Louis Dakeyne, sometimes called Louis the Grand, who bestowed upon himself the pleasing nickname The Exterminator. Louis, by the way, claimed to be the originator of "walking the plank" as a handy means of disposing of his victims.'

'What happened to him at the finish?' asked Dick. 'Did he sun-dry at Execution Dock, like most of the others?'

'As a matter of fact, nobody knows what did become of him,' answered Biggles. 'Speaking from memory, I believe he was the fellow who disappeared just after he had captured a whacking great galleon – much to the relief of every honest sailor engaged in the West Indian trade. I expect he was drowned. Most of the pirates died with their boots on. It's funny to think that some of them may have stood on this very spot, isn't it?'

'Talking of treasure and treasure islands, this must be *our* treasure island, surely, or Deutch wouldn't be here?' suggested Algy.

'I don't think there's much doubt about that,' answered Biggles. 'It struck me as soon as Dick told me that Deutch was here, with our machine, that we had at last reached the place we set out for. What's more, according to the map made by Dick's father, we must be within a quarter of a mile of the old ship he talks about in his letter.' Biggles took the map, which he had recovered from Deutch, from his pocket. 'I made some alterations on it, as I told you,' he continued, 'but in its original form, the cross that marked the position of the ship was up here, at the most northerly point of the island, which is the point immediately opposite to us. This islet we are on is the one marked. We'll go over to the island and have a look round as soon as we've had something to eat, providing Deutch and Co. keep out of the way. It won't do to let them see where we are searching or they'll spot what's afoot and want to join in the fun.'

'Come on, then, let's eat,' cried Dick excitedly.

'We'd better bring the food down here,' suggested Biggles. 'It will be blazing hot on top, in the sun, and Deutch won't be able to see us if we keep below. It will be to our advantage if he doesn't know where we are.'

There was a rush up the stairs, and the stores which they had brought in the canoe, as well as the coconuts Biggles had fetched from the island, were carried below. There was nothing to sit on except the floor, but that did not worry them.

'I don't like the idea of these gentlemen watching us as we eat,' protested Algy with a sidelong glance at the two skeletons.

'They won't hurt us. Dead men don't bite,' retorted Biggles lightly.

While the meal was in progress Algy and Ginger described their adventures, which had ended in their falling into the enemy's hands, after which, for their benefit, Dick told his, describing how he had been rescued by Biggles from Pedro. In this way the time passed quickly, and it was well after midday by the time their hunger was satisfied and the stories told.

Biggles made a little pile of the coconut shells, which they had used as cups after eating their contents. 'Taking it generally, the position has become rather peculiar,' he observed thoughtfully. 'We are here, and Deutch is here, and neither side can get away – at least, not until Harvey comes back with the machine. Where has he gone? Why hasn't he returned? When he first took off I thought, naturally, that he had seen what was happening ashore and was simply concerned with saving the aircraft. Yet if that was the case, one would have expected him to hang around waiting for a chance to get back to the others. Instead, he went straight off as if he was going on an errand; and don't overlook the fact that the course he took up would take him to Marabina – or somewhere near it. I can't help thinking that that is where he has gone. Yet what reason could he have for going back there?'

'He may have gone to fetch some more stores,' suggested Ginger.

'They had ours at their disposal. There must have been ample for their present needs.'

'He may have gone to fetch some tools – shovels and things – to dig for the treasure.'

'Possibly, but knowing the sort of job on which they were engaged, one would have thought that they would have brought such things with them. *We* didn't bring any because we happened to know that they were unnecessary – that is, assuming that the treasure is somewhere in the ship.'

'Do you think Harvey might have lost his nerve and bolted, leaving the others to take care of themselves?' ventured Dick.

'There is just a chance of it, but, somehow, I find that difficult to accept,' returned Biggles shaking his head. 'Men of his stamp don't run away while there is a chance of sharing a treasure. But there, it's no use guessing. If he doesn't come back, then, treasure or no treasure, we're in for a pretty thin time. It's bad enough being marooned on a place like this – for make no mistake, we shall soon get sick of the sight of coconuts when our stores are finished – but when, into the bargain, there's a fellow like 'Frisco Jack prowling about taking pot shots at us, the ordeal is likely to become even more trying. We have only enough food for two or three days at the most; after that we shall have to rely on coconuts.'

'Deutch and Co. will have to do the same thing,' Algy pointed out.

'I know all about that,' agreed Biggles, 'but our position is a very different one from theirs. We should hesitate to shoot them in cold blood, even if we had an opportunity, whereas they'll try to bump us off at the first chance they get.'

'Well, thank goodness one of them is out of action,' declared Dick fervently.

'I thought I'd killed him, but apparently I didn't,' murmured Biggles. 'Still, I fancy he must be pretty sick. Let's go on deck and see what they're up to. Incidentally, from now on we had better mount guards, or they may catch us napping one day.'

'Well, I reckon it's all good fun,' observed Dick optimistically. 'When I read *Treasure Island* at school I never thought the day would come when I'd be on one myself.'

Biggles smiled. 'It's funny, isn't it?' he murmured. 'As a matter of fact, now one comes to think about it, the position here is not unlike the critical situation in the story. Deutch and his confederates are Long John Silver and the pirates, and we—' Biggles grinned delightedly '—why, dash it, it works out exactly. Dick here is Jim Hawkins, Algy is Squire Trelawny, Ginger is Doctor Live-say, and I'm—'

'Captain Smollett,' put in Dick promptly.

Biggles sprang to his feet and bowed. 'At your service, gentlemen. With your assistance we shall yet see Long John Silver – I mean Deutch – sun-drying at Execution Dock. Yes, sir, or my name's not Captain Smollett, and you may lay to that. Avast there! All hands on deck, and step lively, please; let us see what the rascals are at.'

Algy struck a pose. 'By my wig, Captain, you're right, as usual. Stand by for the doubloons.'

They all laughed and then filed up to the roof, from where they could see Pedro still lying on the shore of the lagoon, with Deutch and 'Frisco Jack sitting beside him.

'Don't show yourselves,' warned Biggles.

'Are we going ashore?' inquired Dick excitedly.

Biggles nodded. 'Yes, I think it's safe for us to go and have a look round,' he answered. 'But we had better all be armed. For goodness' sake be careful with these old weapons, though, or we shall have an accident. Dick, is that pistol of yours loaded?'

'No.'

'All right; I'll show you how to load it. Algy – Ginger, you'd better take a musket apiece.'

They went below again where they selected their weapons and loaded them. This done, they returned to the roof and then descended the steps to where the canoe was moored. A few minutes later they were on the island, landing on the rocks of the point, where they lifted the boat into a fissure just above the high-water mark. Satisfied that the coast was clear, they made their way to the top of the headland, where Biggles stopped and surveyed the ground ahead. It was nothing but a matted jungle of bushes, huge cacti, and trailing lianas, and after regarding it for some minutes he shook his head.

'I don't see any galleons lying about, do you?' he asked the others generally.

'It doesn't look the sort of place where you'd expect to find one – at least, not to me,' answered Algy. 'If the wreck is somewhere under this tangle of bushes, then we're in for a long job. It would take an army of men weeks to clear them.'

'Well, let's go and have a look,' replied Biggles. 'I didn't expect to find it with the masts still standing and flags flying; in fact, if you remember, I prophesied that finding the ship was likely to be more difficult than the map might lead one to suppose; but, I must say, now that we are here, it is even worse than I expected. Let's go on for a bit.'

For nearly two hours they searched, thrusting their way into the tangle wherever an opening presented itself, staring about, stamping on the ground, and climbing such elevations as commanded a wider view of the lower ground. Slowly, for it was impossible to move quickly on account of the vegetation, they made their way across the depression that could just be distinguished, until at last they stood on the bare rocks at the far side, where Pedro had overtaken Dick.

Biggles sat down on a boulder and mopped his forehead with his sleeve. 'Phew! This is warm work,' he declared. 'We shall soon have to be getting back; the daylight won't last much longer. We'd better start collecting some nuts to eke out our bully beef, and postpone further operations until tomorrow. In fact, I think it would be a good thing to lay in a good store of nuts while we've got the chance; there are only two or three left in the fort. Dick, go and take a peep over the ridge to make sure the beach is clear. Deutch or 'Frisco may come along, and I'd rather not have a clash if it can be avoided.'

Dick ran off to obey the order, while Ginger and Algy walked towards a little colony of coconut palms that fringed the edge of the jungle not far away; but before they had taken a dozen paces their progress was arrested by Dick, who came dashing back with alarm on his face. 'Look out!' he hissed. ''Frisco and Deutch are coming this way!'

Biggles spun round. 'How far away are they?'

'They are just over the other side of the rock – not more than a stone's throw,' whispered Dick tersely. 'They are creeping along in the shadow of the bushes.'

'Confound them!' Biggles looked annoyed. 'They'll see us as we go across if we try to get to the islet. What a nuisance. I think we'd better get down over the front of the headland and wait by the boat until they go back. Come on, I believe we can get through here.'

With the others following close behind, he led the way at a brisk trot towards a place where the network of briers and lianas appeared to be less dense than usual, in order to reach the far side of the depression previously mentioned, which seemed to stretch from the sea to some distance inland. It was, in fact, the same weak place in the undergrowth that Dick's father had selected as a hiding-place when he had been pursued by Deutch a few months previously, so what followed was not really so much a coincidence as a direct example of cause and effect.

They had almost reached the centre of the depression when Biggles stumbled over a long, round, moss-covered object that lay across their path. 'Hello! What's this?' he muttered, stooping down in order to look along the object for its full length, for it struck him suddenly that it was far too straight and symmetrical to be anything but artificial. It was, in fact, the fallen mainmast of the galleon, and a suspicion of this had just flashed into his mind when Algy, in endeavouring to remove a thorn from his foot, fell forward, and clutched at him for support. Unprepared, Biggles lost his balance, and grabbing wildly at a sapling to save himself, he fell, with Algy on top of him. Instantly there was a loud crack and the ground under them began to sag.

'Look out! The ground's caving in!' gasped Biggles in affright as he struggled to get to his feet. He opened his mouth again to speak, but the words never came. With a soft splintering crash, the rotting, moss-covered timbers of the galleon's deck collapsed, and the next moment they were all precipitated through a gaping hole, landing on the floor, some eight or ten feet lower, with varying degrees of shock.

Biggles was first on his feet, breathing heavily. 'Great Scott! What's happened?' he cried, looking quickly about him. His eyes told him the truth, but even so, he could only stare incredulously, while the others, with groans and mutterings, got up.

'What the—' began Algy, but his astonishment was such that he could get no further.

'I think this is what we've been looking for,' observed Biggles, recovering his self-control as he brushed moss and dirt from his clothes. 'We fell into it, as you might say. I — hark!' He broke off, listening intently.

From not far away came the sound of a human voice. It was Deutch's, and the words reached them clearly. 'I tell you I heard 'em somewhere about here, not a minute ago,' he said.

Biggles laid his finger on his lips warningly. 'Don't speak,' he breathed.

Silently Algy stooped and picked up his musket, which had, of course, fallen in with him. Ginger did the same. Then they all gazed upwards at the breach in the deck through which a shaft of greenish light filtered.

'It must have been a pig, or an animal of some sort,' came 'Frisco's voice doubtfully.

'I tell you I heard 'em talking,' declared Deutch emphatically.

'Then they must have bolted when they heard us coming,' asserted 'Frisco Jack. 'Anyway, there ain't no sense in standing here; the big guy's got a gun, and I don't wanna get plugged through the back, like Pedro. There will be plenty of time to attend to them tomorrow. Let's get back.'

Apparently Deutch acquiesced, for the sound of footsteps, slowly receding, reached the ears of the listeners. Biggles waited for some time to make sure that they had gone before he spoke, but at last he turned to the others. 'Good!' he whispered. 'I think they've gone back. Let's do a bit of exploring.'

Chapter 13

Revelations

Biggles and his companions had not fallen into the galleon in the same place as Dick's father, who had crashed through into the saloon, which, in accordance with the usual practice of the period in which the ship was built, was situated in the poop. They were, as Biggles pointed out, in the fo'castle, which they saw at once was precisely as it had been abandoned, except that what had once been blankets were now mouldering heaps of mildew from which sprouted unhealthy-looking growths of green fungus. Indeed, from them and the few odd articles of clothing that lay about rose an unwholesome stench of corruption and decay. There was little else there of interest except a few weapons, corroded with rust, that had been discarded by the last of the pirates when they had abandoned the ship. Anything of value had been taken with them.

'I don't think we shall find any treasure here,' said Biggles, speaking in an awed whisper, for even he found it impossible not to be affected by the mournful atmosphere of things long dead.

Slowly, almost reverently, they made their way through the waist of the ship, past long-silent cannon, their muzzles half buried in the silt of ages, cannon-balls, powder barrels – some still full – grappling irons – the same that had held the ill-fated *Rose of Bristol* – ropes, blocks, and tackle, all of which they could just see in the eerie light that crept through the cracks in the warping timbers.

'Quite apart from any treasure, this ship ought to be put

into a museum just as it is,' said Biggles quietly. 'I doubt very much if there is another in the same state of preservation in the world, and a lot of people would like to see just how a vessel of this period and class was equipped. I wouldn't have missed it for anything. Unless I am mistaken, we have made a discovery that will cause a sensation at home when it becomes known, particularly among sailors and people interested in the sea.'

Slowly they walked on, staring about them like tourists in the cloisters of an old cathedral. Biggles pointed to a stone jar with a narrow neck, on the bulging sides of which were stamped, in large, black letters, BEST OLD JAMAICA. 'Yo ho ho, and a bottle of rum,' he quoted, singing Stevenson's famous lines with a morbid sort of humour.

Algy nodded thoughtfully as he regarded the old rum puncheon. 'It certainly looks as if "Drink and the devil have done for the rest",' he observed.

They wandered on until at last they came to a companion-way leading upwards. They tested the timbers and, finding them sound, went up. From the top they could see a shaft of pale light falling obliquely across a large room a short distance in front of them. Wonderingly, they made their way towards it, and a moment later they were standing in the captain's saloon, which took up most of the high stern.

Biggles pointed to a jagged hole in the upper deck. Immediately below it lay a quantity of debris, dead moss and the like. 'That, Dick, is where your father must have fallen through,' he said in a low voice.

Dick looked up, fighting to keep back the tears that dimmed his eyes. The fact that his father had stood on the very spot on which he was now standing brought his memory back very clearly. But his grief was short-lived, for there were other things to think of.

141

'Great heavens above! Look at this!' whispered Biggles, in an awe-stricken voice, shaking his head slowly like a man who finds it hard to believe what he sees. The others, looking about them, were too deeply moved for words.

The room was sumptuously furnished. Around the walls, in panels between the gilded lights, were painted pictures of saints and other holy scenes. The whole floor was covered by a magnificent eastern carpet, woven in rich shades of blue and crimson; on it, placed end to end around the outskirts, were several iron-bound chests, with huge, elaborate locks. Most of them were open. Set against the forward bulkhead was a magnificent walnut desk, exquisitely carved, but it was towards a gruesome figure that leaned over it from a high-backed, brass-studded chair, padded with scarlet velvet, that all eyes were irresistibly drawn. It was a skeleton, to which the clothes still clung with dreadful realism.

Biggles, war-hardened, went up to it. A trifle pale, he glanced at the grinning mouth and empty sockets, and then ran his eyes over the details of the clothes. 'This was a Spanish ship,' he said, his voice sounding strangely loud in the eerie silence. 'But this man was no Spaniard; his clothes are more suggestive of a pirate. He must have been the last survivor of some ill-fated crew. What evil fate overtook him, I wonder? What tale of tragedy could he tell if he could speak? It was on this desk that Dick's father found the gold doubloon.' He picked up the silver-mounted pistol, still lying where it had fallen so long ago, and examined it – the first hand to touch it since the pirate's fatal day. 'It has been discharged,' he went on quietly, as if to himself. 'I wonder ... I wonder...' He moved the figure slightly. 'Look!' he said, in a hard, strained voice.

The others came closer to see what had attracted his attention, and this is what they saw. The bony fingers of the skeleton's right hand were pressed to the faded material that still covered the place where the stomach had once been. Under them was a round hole with scorched edges, and a tell-tale stain. Biggles looked down at the floor and caught his breath. His face turned a shade paler. 'Holy smoke!' he breathed, moistening his lips. 'He died by his own pistol. Look!' The others looked down. On the carpet, around the booted feet of the long-dead pirate, was the black, sinister mark that had been made by his drying blood.

'Pretty grim, isn't it?' went on Biggles, recovering some of his self-possession, and moving the skeleton back to its original position. As he did so, something fell heavily to the floor. Almost with repugnance he stooped and picked it up, and holding it between finger and thumb, looked at the others with a curious expression on his face. 'The bullet,' he said. 'The ball that destroyed him. It must have lodged somewhere inside him, and the first movement has shaken it out. Want a souvenir, Dick?'

Dick backed away, an expression of disgust on his face. 'No, thank you,' he said emphatically.

The others laughed, and the spell that had held them in its grip since first they entered the ship was broken.

Biggles stuck the pistol through his belt and pointed to the silver candlestick. 'I should say that's worth a hundred pounds at least,' he observed. 'I wonder if there is anything in these drawers.' He opened the top drawer of the desk. 'Hello! What's this,' he cried, as he took out a leather-bound book. Gently he lifted the cover, and with his eyes turned down inquiringly he studied the first page.

The others saw him start, staring incredulously, lean forward, and stare again. His eyes went round with wonder, and the fingers that held the open page began to tremble slightly. Then, looking up at the faces that were watching him, 'Gentlemen,' he said, in a queer, husky voice, 'allow me to introduce you to the most blood-thirsty member of a bloodthirsty race; the man I spoke about only a short while ago; the self-appointed head of the Brethren of the Coast; cut-throat and murderer – Louis Dakeyne, Louis le Grande, The Exterminator – himself exterminated.'

Dead silence fell, such a silence as had haunted the death-chamber for two hundred and fifty years.

Biggles drew a deep breath. He was finding the experience rather unnerving. 'This is his log,' he said. 'It should make interesting reading. What tales of death, and worse, will it reveal, I wonder? What stories of heroism, until now untold, of lonely mariners fighting their last fight against overwhelming odds led by this fiend in human form? Let us see if we can solve the mystery of his death.' He turned quickly to the last entry in the log, and began to read aloud:

'Rum all out, mutiny aboard, and everything in confusion. Bawn's cursed doubloon the cause, blister him. Put the doubloons overboard, they say. Not me. May the devil seize them first.

'Wind rising again and no-one to take in sail. Murder, mutiny, storm, calm, and out of drink, and now the wind again. The devil himself must be aboard us, and all through Bawn's doubloon, may he rot in his chains at Port Royal. Blast him for a false rogue. The rest have gone to Davy Jones, some by the plank, some by the knife, but I'll . . .'

Biggles broke off breathlessly.

'Is that all?' asked Algy.

'That's all.'

'What was he going to do, I wonder?'

'I'm afraid that is something we will never know. But mark well what he says about Bawn's doubloon. Bawn's *cursed* doubloon. It brought confusion upon them – at least, so he declares. Who Bawn was we do not know, although we may one day find out from the old records that are still kept in Jamaica, but I'll warrant that it was Bawn's doubloon that lay on this desk–'

144

'The doubloon my father took,' interrupted Dick. '*My* doubloon.'

'That's it. I'm not superstitious, but I've felt all along that there was something funny about that coin. It has left a trail of death and disaster behind it. We had no luck while we had it. The only normal luck we've had on this trip was when it was out of our possession. Mallichore took it off us at Marabina. You saw what happened to *him*. We got it back, and you saw what nearly happened to us, and, I honestly believe, would have happened had not Dick discarded his coat, with the doubloon in the pocket, at the last minute. The coat was washed up. Algy and Ginger found it. Within half an hour they were face to face with death. At the crucial moment Pedro took the coin, and the evil influence went with it. I shot him within the hour. To the long list of casualties I think we can now add the names of Louis le Grande and his crew.'

'He talks of other doubloons,' reminded Algy.

'I know, and what happened here is now as clear as daylight,' returned Biggles swiftly. 'Dakeyne's crew knew the cursed doubloon was aboard, and wanted to get rid of it. He says so in his log. But somehow it had got mixed up with the others, and Louis wouldn't jettison the lot.'

'He must have done at the finish – or else they're still aboard,' asserted Algy.

'Aboard or ashore, I should say they're not far away from us at this moment,' declared Biggles.

'Where could they be?' cried Dick.

Biggles shrugged his shoulders. 'That's what we've got to find out. I believe Dakeyne was in the act of making a map of the hiding-place when he was killed. Dick's father found the paper on his desk. I've got it in my pocket. I haven't been able to make head nor tail of it, but now we are actually on the spot I will have another look at it.' He picked up the quill that still lay on the desk. 'Here is the pen

145

he used,' he said, glancing up at the sky, just visible through the breach in the deck. 'We shall have to be getting back,' he went on quickly. 'It will be dark in another quarter of an hour, so we've no time for doubloon-hunting today, unless they happen to be handy, which seems doubtful. We've just time for a quick look round.'

The other drawers in the desk yielded three items of interest. In one lay what appeared to be a black tablecloth, neatly folded. Biggles was about to pass it over, and had half closed the drawer when a thought seemed to strike him. He reopened the drawer, took out the black material and, with a quick movement, shook it open. At once it became a flag, complete with loops for a lanyard – a black flag; a field of black with a white device, the device being a skeleton, holding, upraised, in its right hand, a dart; in the other, an hour-glass. Each foot rested on an initial letter. They read L D.

'By the red beard of Barbarossa!' exclaimed Biggles, 'fate has played a grim jest here. On the flag is Death, standing on the initials of the man who flew it; and here in the chair is death itself – the mortal remains of the same man. What a pity he can't return from the shades, if only for a moment, to see the joke.' Biggles tossed the flag to Dick. 'Bring it along,' he said. 'It's a unique trophy.'

In another drawer was a magnificent ruby ring, which Biggles slipped into his pocket with the casual observation that it seemed a pity to leave it lying about. In another were about a hundred silver coins. 'Pieces of eight,' he said laconically, picking one up and examining it. 'Find a bag or something to carry them in, Ginger. We had better take them with us in case Deutch happens to find the ship, which is by no means improbable if he starts crashing about in the bushes up above, looking for us.'

They made a quick examination of the chests, but they were all full of bolts of silks, satins, and other fine materials in which moths or other insects had played havoc, destroying their value. Afterwards they looked into the hold, but they found nothing more interesting than a number of barrels more or less full of mouldering sugar, coffee, and flour.

They would have liked to stay longer, for there were still many places to explore, but Biggles pointed to the darkening sky and ordered a retreat. 'Without any sort of illumination it isn't much use staying here,' he remarked. 'Moreover, I've no desire to spend the night with Louis. Let's get back to the islet; all being well, we can return first thing in the morning.'

But this was easier said than done, for they could find no means of regaining the hole through which they had fallen. Algy tried standing on Biggles's shoulders, but the rotten timber crumbled under his hands as soon as he put his weight on it, and they had to abandon the project. They began to understand the difficulty that Dick's father had experienced. In the end they found the hole he had made in the bows, and picking up their trophies, they crawled one by one out of the dim past into the twilit world of the present.

The boat was as they had left it, so, putting it on the water, they paddled back to the islet, and the fort which they had made their home.

'We'll make an early start in the morning,' declared Biggles as they enjoyed a frugal meal from their fast dwindling stores, helped by the remaining coconuts which provided both food and drink. 'But before we do any serious treasure-hunting,' he went on, 'I think it would be a wise move if we put this place in a better state to stand a siege. Sooner or later, whether Harvey comes back or not, Deutch and 'Frisco are bound to locate us, and if they decide to move their camp to the rocks opposite, 'Frisco, with his gun, would make it very awkward for us to get to and fro.

We'll lay in a supply of coconuts, and bring some more gunpowder over. We may need it if it comes to a showdown. If 'Frisco starts any rough stuff we could give him a dose of grape-shot,* which should make him think a bit. Another thing we shall have to do is mount guards. In fact, we had better start now; we should look a lot of fools if we let them catch us napping. A two-hour shift for everyone will see us through until morning. I think I'll just have another look at Dakeyne's map – if it is a map.'

He went over to one of the loopholes and spread the piece of yellow paper flat against a stone, where they all looked at it for a long time. At last Biggles shook his head. 'It must mean something,' he said. 'But if you can tell me what it is you're cleverer than I am.'

The others agreed that they could make nothing of it, so Biggles folded the paper and put it back into his pocket. 'I think we can do without those two unpleasant-looking fellows,' he said, pointing to the skeletons. 'It's time they went to Davy Jones, where they belong. Bear a hand everybody, to heave them overboard.'

The gruesome job was soon done, and Biggles turned to Dick. 'You'd better take the first watch,' he said. 'It's the easiest. Wake Ginger when the moon shows clear above the palms; that will be roughly in two hours' time.'

'Ay, ay, sir,' replied Dick briskly, and made his way up to the roof.

* Small metal balls put together in a bag and fired from a cannon, often with devastating effect.

Chapter 14

Dick Goes Ashore

For what seemed a long time Dick sat alone on the roof. At first he could hear the others talking down below, but after a while their conversation became intermittent, and then finally stopped altogether, so he assumed that they were sleeping. Silence fell, the breathless hush of a tropic night. The quivering of the palm fronds ceased, and even the gentle lap, lap, lap, of the ripples at the foot of the rock died away. The stars shone in the heavens with unbelievable luminosity, like lamps suspended from a purple ceiling. The moon crept over the horizon and began its upward journey, turning the sea into a lake of shimmering quicksilver, and the island into a mysterious world of vague black shadows. Across the deserted beach the black rocks crouched like monsters emerging from the ocean bed.

Dick leaned his musket against the rampart wall and regarded the scene with questioning, brooding eyes. It produced a queer sensation to think that on the very spot, wearing the same clothes and armed with the same weapons, an Elizabethan sentinel may have stood, doing sentry just as he was doing it now. Perhaps the gallant Drake himself had been there! Afterwards had come the buccaneers – the pirates. They must have known of the little fort, and used the creek, perhaps careened their ships on the coral strand inside the shelter of the headland. With all their lust and cruelty, they must have been romantic days in which to live; vaguely, he was sorry that they had gone. Treasure or no treasure, he would, he knew, rather have been a member of Drake's stalwart crew, or even Dakeyne's, than sell papers in a London street. Louis le Grande! He whispered the words, rolling them off his tongue with relish. What days they were, when new lands remained to be discovered! What men they bred! What ships they built! Dimly, he perceived that although the days were gone the men remained, and many there were in town and city who would go back to them if they could.

A feeling of intense depression swept over him, for he knew that the gallant days of sail had gone for ever. Men themselves had done it; condemned themselves for ever to be slaves of iron and steel. What fools they were! To satisfy their longing, they messed about with little ships, around the harbours, at weekends. There was no romance in smoking funnels; his father had often told him so, and he realized it now. The voice of the throbbing screw had silenced for ever the creak of blocks, and the song of the breeze through straining sheets. The risks had gone, and with them, the joy of victory over them. Yes, it was a great pity, he reflected sadly.

Yet life was not so bad, after all, for he was luckier than most. Was it not true that within a short distance of where he stood a pirate's hoard remained? Doubloons! He said the word aloud. How much more satisfying it sounded than 'pound notes'. Paper money. Pah! What inspiration was there in paper? Thank goodness they weren't looking for a parcel of paper notes. Gold! That was the stuff. Solid metal with a healthy ring to it, not a feeble crackle, like notes. No wonder men went a-pirating when they used such money as that. Dakeyne must have collected quantities. Where was it now? Where had he put the doubloons? If he had buried them, how could they hope to find them? As Biggles had said, it would need an army of men to turn over all the rock and sand within a quarter of a mile of the galleon. It was a pity that Louis le Grande had not been more concise, had not finished the map he was making. He could still visualize the paper, but he could not associate it with anything he had seen. Were they on the wrong track after all? Suppose the lines on the slip of paper were just meaningless marks made by a dying man? It might well be so. In that case the secret of the treasure might still remain where he had hidden it. There was nothing in the candlestick, for Biggles had looked to see. What else was there an the desk? The pistol. There was nothing in that. The quill offered little hope. The doubloon! Louis might have scratched a message on the coin. They had not examined it very closely. That was the sort of thing a pirate might do, he reflected. What a pity Biggles had kicked it into the hole.

The more he thought about it the more he wished he had examined it more closely. In view of what he now knew, he would look at it through different eyes. What a triumph it would be if he solved the mystery where the others had failed! It would be a feather in his cap. How foolish it had been of Biggles to throw the coin away. He shouldn't have done it. After all, it was *his* coin.

The desire to examine it again for the marks he had now almost convinced himself were on it, became a mania, and he began to look towards the spot where it had been discarded. Another thought struck him. After all, it wasn't very far away. He might fetch it. There was nothing to prevent him. He could get into the boat and be there and back in ten minutes at the very outside. Nothing could happen in that time, he persuaded himself, although in his heart of hearts he knew that he had no right to leave his post. But everything was very quiet, and it was hard to believe that anything could happen before he got back.

At the end be made up his mind quickly, although somewhat guiltily. He crept to the top of the stairs that led down to the room where the others slept. All was quiet. He tiptoed back to the wall. Then, leaving his musket, but examining his pistol to make sure it was primed, he went quickly down the outside steps that led to the sea. In another minute he was in the canoe, paddling swiftly but silently towards the point.

He landed where they had gone ashore a few hours earlier, and tying the boat to a convenient crag, made his way swiftly up the rock. Reaching the top, he paused to look round. All was silent – rather too silent for his liking. In some queer way it reminded him of the silence in the galleon. Louis le Grande! He hoped his spirit did not walk. He shook himself angrily. What made him think about these things now? He had come to fetch the doubloon, but it was not so easy as he had thought it would be when he was standing on the islet with the others only a few yards away. He braced himself suddenly, annoyed by his nervousness. 'Dead men don't bite,' he muttered angrily, and set off towards the hole into which Biggles had kicked the coin, the hole in which he had nearly lost his life at the hands of the dreadful Pedro. He sped on, throwing furtive glances at the unexpected shadows cast by the moonlight. Some of them looked very human.

With his heart beating faster than usual he reached the hole. A swift glance around and he had dropped into it, palms feeling lightly for the metal disk. He found it almost at once; with a gasp of relief his hand closed over it; and then, and not before, did he remember the superstition of the curse. Half fearfully, as though he could not bear to touch it more than he could help, he stood upright, and pushed the coin on to a flat piece of rock in order to free his hands while he climbed out.

Resting them on the ledge, he vaulted up, but his pistol caught on a jagged piece of rock and threw him back. More annoying still, for he was anxious to be gone, the weapon was pulled clean out of his belt and clattered to the bottom of the hole. With a muttered imprecation, for he dare not go without it, he dropped on to his hands and knees, groping swiftly, for the moonbeams fell aslant, and did not penetrate to where the pistol lay.

His questing hand closed over something, and as he felt its shape he stiffened, rigid, tense. Surely it was the doubloon! It felt just like it. But he had already put it outside! There could not be two. Could it have fallen back inside? Swiftly he stood up and looked over the ledge of rock on which he had put the coin. It was still there, gleaming softly in the moonlight. There could be no mistake. Then what was it he held in his hand? He opened it to see. It was a doubloon. Then there *were* two! But that was impossible! How...? He began to tremble, and perspiration broke out on his forehead as his superstitious fears returned in force. The thing must be bewitched. What a fool he had been ever to touch it again – unless?

He caught his breath as another thought flashed into his brain. Quickly he stooped again, fingers scooping at the bottom of the hole. They closed over a handful of small round objects, and his mouth went dry as he felt their shape. Hardly able to breathe, he leaned against the side of the rock, and opening his trembling hand, stared wide-eyed at what it held! Doubloons! A dozen or more of them. He scraped with his foot, and heard the metallic ring of others. He was standing on doubloons! He had found Dakeyne's doubloons ... *The* doubloons! The words seemed to ring in his ears. He forgot his pistol. He even forgot where he was and what he was doing. Breathing fast, again he dropped to his knees, fingers clawed. They sank into the golden pile. Were they really there, or was it all a dream? He felt again. No, it was no dream; they were real enough. He must tell the others about it at once.

Leaving the coins where they were, for without pockets he had no means of carrying them, he was about to leap joyfully out of the hole when a sound reached his ears that sent him cowering to the bottom again, his heart beating as though it would choke him, while his body turned as cold as the stones by which he crouched. It was the sound of a human voice, and there was no mistaking the guttural tones. The speaker was Deutch.

'I tell you they're round this headland somewhere,' he said in a surly voice.

'Aw shucks! What does it matter, anyway?' replied the voice of 'Frisco Jack. 'What's the hurry? There ain't no call to get nervy. We'll round the lot of 'em up tomorrow and bump 'em off.'

'I'd like to know what they're up to,' replied Deutch with an oath. Then he spoke again, in a voice charged with interest. 'What's that over there?'

Dick nearly swooned as rapid footsteps approached the hole; they seemed to stop on the very edge, and he braced himself for the blow which he felt was coming. But he did not move – possibly because it was beyond his physical strength to do so.

'Why, if it ain't the gold buck,' came 'Frisco's voice, tense with surprise. 'Now what do you make 'o that?'

'Blister their hides! They must have found the doubloons, and dropped one, or how else did this one git here?'

'Beats me!' murmured 'Frisco. 'Hold hard,' he went on quickly. 'I've got it. This is where Pedro got plugged. He had the doubloon, you recollect. He must 'a dropped it when he fell. That's it. This is where I found 'im. Look, there's his blood marks. Well, he's gone where doubloons won't be no use to 'im, so I might as well have it.'

'Hands off, 'Frisco! I found it; it's mine.' Deutch's voice had a hard, vindictive ring.

Came the American's voice again, bitter in its frigid hostility. 'Hey, what's biting you, Deutch?'

'Hand it over,' snarled Deutch, from which Dick,

shivering with horror in the hole, gathered that the American had picked up the coin.

'Frisco spoke again, fury blazing in his clipped words. 'You dirty rat! Pull a knife on me, would you, you—' His voice broke off in a choking gasp that ended in a horrid gurgling sound. There was a swishing and writhing on the rocks, punctuated with grunts accompanied by the sound of fiercely driven blows. Then silence.

Dick bit his lip to prevent himself from crying out aloud. He could visualize what was happening on the very edge of his hiding place. In a nightmare of horror he heard Deutch muttering, between deeply drawn breaths, 'I'll teach you, you—' each sentence concluding with an oath worse than the last.

At last, to Dick's unspeakable relief, the footsteps began to recede, but it was a good ten minutes before he dare move from his cramped position. Slowly he drew himself upright. His face, in the pallid moonlight, was ashen, but he did not know it. One glance was enough. His fears were realized. A yard or two away, the wan light shining whitely on his death-distorted features, lay 'Frisco Jack.

Dick did not wait to collect any doubloons. He did not stop to pick up his pistol. He waited for nothing. One leap and he was out of the hole, running for dear life towards the rock where he had left the boat. Several times he nearly fell, for his knees were strangely weak. He literally tumbled into the boat, and untying the painter with trembling hands, snatched up the paddle and sent it flashing through the water. Panting with excitement and exertion, he crossed the narrow channel, moored the boat – not without difficulty, so violently did he tremble – and dashed up the steps to the fort. He could hear the others talking before he reached the top. Apparently they heard him coming, for Biggles's voice, as hard as cracking ice, came down to him below the rampart wall.

'Halt there! Who goes?'

'It's me,' gasped Dick.

'All right; come aboard.'

Dick finished his journey. At the top he found Biggles waiting for him. His eyes were cold and his manner hostile. The others stood close behind him. 'Where the devil have you been?' he snapped.

Dick faltered. 'I've been ashore,' he panted. 'I've found—'

Biggles's voice cut in, crisp and curt. 'Never mind what you've found. You left your post!'

'But—'

'I don't want any excuses. Did you, or did you not, leave your post?'

'Yes, sir.'

'Then you ought to be thundering well ashamed of yourself. Are you?'

'Yes, sir.'

'Well, that's something, anyway. Fortunately no harm came of it, but if you ever do that again I'll tie a couple of cannon-balls to your feet and throw you overboard. Orders are orders – you understand?'

'Yes, sir.'

'Why did you do it?'

'I went to fetch the doubloon.'

Biggles took a quick pace backward. 'You *what?*'

'You see, I thought—'

'Wait a minute – wait a minute. Have you brought that accursed coin back here? If you have, you can take it ashore again, and as soon as you like, my lad.'

'No, Deutch has got it.'

'How do you know that?'

'He and 'Frisco were over there. I got into the hole and found the doubloon and put it on a rock while I got out. I bobbed down again when Deutch and 'Frisco came along. Deutch spotted the doubloon, but 'Frisco got it first and wouldn't give it up. They fought to see who should have it, and in the end Deutch knifed 'Frisco. He's lying over there on the rocks, dead. Deutch has gone off with the doubloon.'

Biggles turned to the others. His manner was slow and deliberate. 'Did you hear that?' he said in a strange voice. 'Another death to the score of Bawn's doubloon. By heavens, there's more than coincidence in this! Deutch is welcome to it; he's sealed his own fate or I've missed my mark.' He turned back to Dick. 'What were you doing all this time?'

'I was lying in the bottom of the hole; you see, I'd just found some more.'

'Some more what?'

'Doubloons.'

There was a brief silence. Biggles spoke. 'Did you say you'd found some more doubloons?' he asked incredulously.

'Yes.'

'How many?'

'Hundreds – maybe thousands,' declared Dick exultantly.

'Are you sure?'

'Certain! I held them in my hands.'

Biggles eyed Dick suspiciously. 'You didn't by any chance drop off to sleep and dream this, did you?'

Dick took a pace forward. 'Sleep!' he cried. 'I did not. I was scared stiff. I tell you I picked up the doubloons in handfuls.'

Biggles turned again to the others. 'Jumping alligators! He must have found the treasure,' he breathed. Then to Dick, 'Where is it?'

'In the hole where you kicked the doubloon – the same hole where I hid when Pedro was after me. We stood beside it this afternoon.'

Biggles rubbed his chin. 'Would you believe it?' he murmured. 'So *that's* where Louis dumped them when his ship ran into the creek? And after all this time Bawn's doubloon got back amongst the others. There seems to be a sort of fate in this.' A light of understanding came suddenly into his eyes. 'Why, what fools we were!' he cried. 'I see it all now, although I should never have guessed it. Those two parallel lines on Louis's map were the boundaries of the inlet, with the holes in the rocks marked beside it. The one in which he put the gold was filled in solid. Well, well, it's easy to be wise after the event. What were Deutch and 'Frisco doing up there, Dick?'

'Looking for us, and talking.'

'Could you hear what they were saying?'

'They didn't say very much, but they were talking about rounding us up tomorrow and bumping us off.'

Biggles inclined his head. 'How very nice of them. Did they say just how they proposed to do that?'

'No, but they seemed pretty confident. They talked as if something was due to happen tomorrow that would make it easy.'

Biggles looked thoughtful. 'I don't quite see how that can be,' he said slowly, 'but it's as well to know what was in their minds. I should have thought that the boot was on the other foot. We were four against two; now we are four against one, assuming that Pedro is out of action.'

'He's dead,' put in Dick quickly. 'At least, I heard 'Frisco say that he had gone where doubloons wouldn't be much good to him.'

'Another victim to the doubloon,' said Biggles softly. 'Where is 'Frisco now, Dick?'

'He's lying over there beside the hole.'

'Then we'd better move him first thing in the morning, in case Deutch comes prowling about and finds the treasure – not that I think we have much to fear from him now. We can't do much in the dark, but we'll get busy as soon as it starts to get light; meanwhile, we'd better see about getting some rest. Ginger, take over guard, and don't go wandering ashore; you may not be so lucky as Dick was.'

Dick smiled at the faint sarcasm in Biggles's voice as he followed the others below and lay down to try to get some sleep. But it was a long time coming, and when at length it came he was haunted by dreams in which Dakeyne, Deutch, 'Frisco Jack, and the doubloons were hopelessly interwoven.

Chapter 15

The Attack

He awoke with a start, aware that he had slept. It was still dark, but he could see a vague form moving about the room. He sat up to see more clearly.

It was Biggles who, seeing him move, addressed him. 'Parade in five minutes. Full marching order.'

'It's very early, isn't it?'

'In these parts, it's the early buccaneer who catches the doubloons,' answered Biggles lightly. 'The stars are paling. Dawn will break in about five minutes. Hey, there, Ginger, show a leg! I want to get ashore before Deutch starts prowling about. Crack yourselves a nut apiece for breakfast.'

Ginger sat up, yawning. 'What the dickens have you been doing?' he inquired sleepily.

'Giving the battery the once-over; in other words, inspecting the guns.'

'Do you think we are likely to need them?'

'One never knows what one is likely to need when one goes a-pirating.'

'Where's Algy?'

'On the roof; doing guard and finishing his brekker. Jump to it; we go ashore in three minutes.'

Ginger sprang to his feet. 'My goodness, I'd forgotten about the doubloons! Are we going to fetch them?'

'We are. We should look a lot of silly asses if, having found them, Deutch found them, too, and hid them in another place. I'd rather they were under my eye. Ready?'

Ginger cracked a nut, took a quick drink of the milk, and breaking off a piece of the kernel, handed it to Dick. 'Ay, ay, sir,' he said.

'Then all aboard for the dollars. We've a lot to do today.'

Algy joined them at the top of the stairs. Already the sky was pale azure blue, with the rim of the sun just showing above the horizon. They could just see the lagoon, but there was no sign of Deutch, or the amphibian, from which they concluded that Harvey had not yet returned; so, each carrying a loaded musket, they made their way down the outside steps to the canoe.

In five minutes they were across, with their frail craft made fast.

'Dick and Ginger, stand fast,' ordered Biggles. 'Algy, come with me.'

'What's the idea?' inquired Dick.

'We've got a job to do. We'll call you as soon as it's done,' answered Biggles seriously. 'Come on, Algy.'

Dick sat down on a convenient piece of rock. He realized what the job was. A few minutes later he breathed a sigh of relief as he heard a loud splash on the far side of the headland, knowing that it was done. He had no desire to see 'Frisco again. 'Queer, isn't it?' he said to Ginger, who was sitting beside him. 'Gold always seems to be associated with dead men.'

'Because too many of the wrong sort of men try to get hold of it, I expect,' returned Ginger philosophically.

A hail from Biggles sent them hurrying up the rock, where they found him and Algy waiting for them.

'Now, Dick,' said Biggles, 'you found the doubloons, so it's only right and proper that you should lead us to the spot.'

With shining eyes Dick led the way to the hole in which he had twice taken refuge. 'There they are,' he said, pointing.

'My goodness! He's right,' declared Biggles, staring down into the hole.

They all laughed, a trifle hysterically.

Biggles jumped down and picked up a handful of doubloons. 'You're right, Dick,' he said, rather breathlessly. 'There must be thousands of them.'

'Let's take them across and count them,' suggested Dick.

Biggles climbed up out of the hole. 'Wait a minute,' he said. 'We mustn't lose our heads. If we take them across to the islet it means that we shall have to make that our headquarters, perhaps for a long time, in which case my common sense tells me that we ought to provision it. A rough sea might prevent us from crossing over here for days on end, and we should look a lot of silly asses sitting on a pile of gold with nothing to eat. We've got the day before us, so we may as well take things in order. Ginger, you collect a pile of nuts and carry them across. Algy, you go down into the galleon and find a way of getting some gunpowder to the boat for Ginger to ship across. We may need our muskets, and there isn't much powder over there. Dick, you go with him and fetch one of those old water-buckets. There are several lying about beside the cannon: they used to use them for carrying water to sluice out the guns. Bring it back here and we'll use it to transport the doubloons. I'll start getting them out of the hole.'

'What about Deutch?' asked Ginger.

'I think he will have more sense than to take on the four of us,' returned Biggles casually. 'But if he comes along looking for trouble he can have it. With that doubloon in his pocket he's as good as dead already. All right. Go to it, everybody.'

By the time the sun was well up the first part of their task was complete, and Algy and Ginger joined Biggles and Dick at the treasure hole.

'Got some nuts across, Ginger?' asked Biggles.

'Yes.'

'How about powder, Algy?'

'I've taken over the best part of a barrel; that should be enough to last us for a long time.'

'Good enough,' declared Biggles. 'All hands to ship the doubloons. I've only got about half of them out of the hole; they're heavier than you would believe. I think the best way to go to work is for you, Algy, and Ginger, to start shipping them across to the fort while Dick and I go on hauling them up.'

The shipment of the coins was a task to their liking, and they went to work with a will; but even so it took them longer than they expected, although, with most of the afternoon still before them, they were not particularly concerned with time. However, when at last the job was done, and they tossed into the bucket the last few coins that remained, Biggles estimated that between forty and fifty thousand doubloons, moidores, and ducats, with a sprinkling of oriental pieces, had been carried across to the fort.

'What you might call a good day's work,' he grinned, mopping the perspiration from his face. 'We'll take these last few across and have a rest; afterwards we'll decide what to do about Deutch. He's keeping very quiet, by the way. Dick, run up to the ridge and see if you can see anything of him.'

He sat down near the others while Dick ran lightly up the barrier of rock that lay at right angles across the beach and obstructed their view in the direction of the lagoon.

Lightheartedly – he even stopped to examine a queer shaped shell on the way – Dick reached the ridge and glanced nonchalantly along the beach. For a moment he stared, thunderstruck into immobility, hardly able to believe his eyes; then he whirled round and raced back towards the others, leaping from rock to rock in a manner that was reckless, if not dangerous. And as he ran he shouted.

'Look out!' he yelled. 'Run for it! Quick!' He swerved towards the place where the boat was moored.

The others sprang to their feet in alarm. 'What is it?' cried Biggles.

'Soldiers! The soldiers from Marabina. Dozens of them,' answered Dick in a panic. 'They're coming this way, and they're only just over the other side of the rocks.'

Biggles waited for no more. He snatched up his musket and made a grab at the bucket that contained the remaining doubloons, but Algy, in his haste, tripped over it, and sent the yellow coins flying in all directions. Muttering at his carelessness, he started to pick them up, but Biggles made him desist.

'Never mind those,' he snapped. 'They are not worth stopping for. Down to the boat – come on.'

To the boat they dashed, pell-mell, infected by the panic in Dick's manner. Having got a flying start, he raced them to it, and was ready, paddle in hand, by the time they arrived. There was a wild scramble for places. Biggles snatched the paddle out of Dick's hands, used it to thrust the canoe clear, and then drove it deep into the water. Simultaneously, a chorus of yells from the top of the rocks told them that they had been seen. There was a moment's silence and then more excited shouts.

'They've found the doubloons we spilt,' grunted Biggles, as he put his weight behind the paddle.

He was right, and although he, and the others in the canoe, may not have realized it, the trivial incident of Algy accidentally upsetting the bucket may have saved their lives. Several of the soldiers were in the act of levelling their rifles when an astonished cry from one of their number attracted their attention to the coins. Some started to pick them up, whereupon those who were about to shoot – and the range was then point blank – seeing that they were likely to lose their share, threw down their rifles and joined in the mad scramble. Not even Deutch's furious cursing could stop them, and by the time they were satisfied that no more gold remained, the canoe was three parts of the way to the islet.

Deutch threw up the automatic he had taken from 'Frisco Jack and blazed away, but what with rage and exertion his aim was wild, and the bullets splashed harmlessly on the water. Some of the soldiers then fired, and one or two bullets came close enough to splash water into the canoe.

'Take a shot at them, Algy,' panted Biggles. 'It will rattle them even if you don't hit anybody.'

Algy's musket roared, and the vicious thud of the ball on the rocks had the desired effect. The soldiers dived for cover. They began firing again almost at once, but the brief respite had enabled Biggles to run the canoe alongside the landing place, where it was under the protection of the steps.

'Up you go,' cried Biggles. 'One at a time.'

For two or three seconds, as they crossed a shoulder of the rock, they again came into the field of fire of the watchers on the point, but they ran the gauntlet successfully. Biggles was the last, for he had had to make the canoe fast. 'Phew!' he muttered, as he dropped over the wall and crouched beside the others. 'That was warm work. Where the deuce did that mob come from?'

He crawled across to a loophole on the opposite side of the ramparts, one that overlooked the lagoon. His face was grave as he turned back to Algy. 'This is not so good,' he said seriously.

'What is it?'

'A boat. Looks like a sort of coastal craft, about the size of a trawler. Possibly it's a coastguard. What the dickens brought it here, I wonder? I've got it,' he went on quickly. 'Harvey! He went back to Marabina and told them we were here, and they've sent the boat after us. Either that, or Deutch asked for extra help to find the doubloons. Those thieving officials at Marabina are in on the deal.'

'That's it,' agreed Algy. 'The fellow in the pretty uniform is here with them; I saw him as we came across.'

'How many of them are there, do you think?'

'There can't be less than a score – probably more.'

'That's how I figured it out. It looks as if it's a good thing we laid a few nuts in store, doesn't it? Hark!'

'There he is! It must be Harvey coming back,' cried Ginger. He pointed to a speck far out to sea, to the south-west.

'Yes, that's our machine,' said Biggles, shielding his eyes with his hand. 'It looks as if we've a tidy force opposed to us.'

Keeping under cover of the rampart wall, they watched the machine land, and then, peeping through various loopholes, they looked back at the point. The troops had withdrawn some distance, but they could see them being addressed by Deutch in the shade of the jungle.

'Hello! What's he going to do?' asked Biggles suddenly.

'Looks like a flag of truce,' answered Algy in a surprised voice.

With a dirty piece of white rag held high on a stick, Deutch advanced to the nearest point of the rock. 'Hi, you over there,' he bellowed.

Biggles spoke sharply to Algy. 'Keep me covered,' he said. 'Let drive at the first sign of dirty work.' Then he stood up. 'Hello yourself,' he answered.

'I've come to offer you a square deal,' shouted Deutch.

'What's your idea of a square deal?'

'You show us where you've hid the dough and we'll give you a passage back to Marabina.'

Biggles smiled. 'Thanks,' he called sarcastically. 'We'd sooner be where we are.'

'You mean you won't show us where you've hid the dibs?'

'Not a mother's son of 'em.'

'All right, my cock. You won't chirp so loud by the time I'm through with you; maybe I can find a way of making you talk.'

'Not forgetting that you've got to catch me first.'

Deutch cursed vindictively. 'I'll skin you alive when I lay hands on you,' he roared as he turned away, shaking his clenched fist. He rejoined the troops, and a minute later two or three detached themselves and set off at a run down the beach.

'I wonder what they're going to do?' murmured Algy.

'I should say they're going to fetch a boat from the coaster,' returned Biggles. 'They'll bring it back here and then try to storm us. I'm afraid we're in for a sticky time, but our only chance is to fight it out. Well, whatever happens, Deutch isn't getting those.' He pointed to the heap of doubloons that gleamed dully in a corner. 'If the worst comes to the worst, I'll heave the whole lot into the sea rather than he should get his hands on them. Come on, let's get busy and load every weapon we've got. We've a good card up our sleeves and we'll keep it there as long as we can. Deutch knows we've got muskets, but he doesn't know about these babies.' He touched one of the cannon with his toe. Then he smiled. 'As a soldier I've always been curious to see the effect of a charge of grape-shot, and it looks as if this is my chance,' he observed. 'Let's get the swivel-gun up here; I've got a feeling that it is going to upset Mr Deutch's calculations.'

'How can we fire the guns?' asked Algy suddenly. 'We haven't a match between us.'

'We can soon get over that difficulty,' answered Biggles promptly. 'When we're ready I'll snap a pistol into some loose powder with some pieces of dry rag in it. We shall have to keep a little fire going.

The sun blazed down as they rammed the powder into the guns. Algy picked up a cannon ball weighing perhaps five pounds. 'If this happens to hit anybody in the teeth there'll be no need for him to see a dentist,' he declared cheerfully, as he thrust it into a yawning muzzle.

The swivel-gun was dragged up from below, and with perspiration streaming from them, they aligned it on the channel. All the powder, shot, and small arms, including another cutlass and a pike, were brought up, and placed in handy positions. When it was done Biggles nodded approval as he glanced round. 'Well,' he observed, 'they may take us, but before they do there will be such a noise as should cheer the mouldering bones of Louis le Grande. By gosh! I'll tell you what! We'll fly his flag. It's many a day since the Jolly Roger flapped over the Main, and if it never flaps again we'll be the last to fly it.' He ran below and returned with the grim emblem of piracy. He picked up the pike, and after tying the flag to it, wedged the handle into the draining hole in the corner.

Dick regarded it with shining eyes. 'That's the stuff!' he cried approvingly. Then he burst into song:

> 'Fifteen men on the dead man's chest,
> Yo ho ho, and a bottle of rum.'

The others joined in the famous refrain, roaring it at the top of their voices.

> 'Drink and the devil had done for the rest,
> Yo ho ho, and a bottle of rum.'

Algy, looking through his loophole, saw the astonished faces of the soldiers peering out of the jungle. 'They think we've gone crazy,' he declared.

Biggles nodded. 'They're not far wrong, either,' he murmured drily. Then his eyes glinted. 'Avast there, pipe down,' he cried. 'Here comes the boat.'

A small boat had appeared from the direction of the lagoon; it was being rowed by four men, who kept close into the shore. It disappeared behind the headland, and presently the watchers, from their eyrie, saw Deutch's crew creeping down towards it.

'How many men can they get into that boat?' asked Algy.

'Not more than a dozen,' replied Biggles shortly. 'Here they come,' he added quickly, as the boat shot round the end of the point. It was low in the water under the weight of the men crowded into it. Four were rowing, urged on by Deutch who sat in the stern.

'Hold your fire until I give the word,' ordered Biggles.

He waited until the boat was half way across. Then, 'Fire!' he roared.

The four muskets blazed, their booming reports echoing again and again in the hills. Water splashed round the boat. A man collapsed, but the rowers continued to ply their oars. Biggles snatched up another musket. 'Rapid fire!' he yelled.

Under the fusillade of musketry, two more of the soldiers collapsed, one springing up and falling overboard; but the boat still surged towards the islet.

Biggles leapt to the brass swivel-gun, snatching up a piece of smouldering rag from the fire he had lighted for the purpose. There was a curious smile on his face as he brought the long barrel to bear. He dropped some loose powder on the touch-hole; then leapt aside as he fired it with the rag. A stream of flame and sparks spurted from the muzzle as the gun roared; a great cloud of smoke bellied outwards.

Had Biggles been serious when he said that he wanted to see the result of grape-shot, his wish was fulfilled. And it exceeded anything he imagined. In the first place, the recoil was terrific. He had rammed probably a hundred bullets into the gun. They struck the boat, and the water around it, in a murderous hail of lead. The water was churned into foam for an area of several square yards. The boat nearly overturned. Shouts and groans rose on the air. Inside the boat all was chaos. Only one of the rowers retained his oars, and these he was unable to use because of the turmoil. Above the uproar rose the frenzied cursing of Deutch. The bows of the boat, seemingly of their own volition, turned back towards the shore. The rower got his oars free and recommenced rowing furiously. A soldier snatched up another oar and helped him, using it as a paddle.

Biggles barely saw these things, for he was working like a madman reloading the gun. By the time he had finished the boat had nearly reached the sand near the point, but pressing home his advantage, he snatched up another piece of rag and fired the touch.

Boom! Another great cloud of smoke rolled turgidly towards the island.

When it had cleared somewhat they saw that the boat had overturned, and was lying awash in the gentle ripples on the beach. Two or three men were splashing in the water; others floated motion less. One was crawling up the sand. Three or four others, Deutch among them, were running for cover, and presently disappeared behind the rocks.

'Go on firing at the boat,' shouted Biggles. 'Try to knock some holes in her bottom.' Suiting the action to the word, he snatched up an undischarged musket and fired. A splinter of wood leapt from the upturned keel. Reloading, he fired again. For another five minutes they continued the fusillade before he gave the order to cease fire. 'That's given them something to think about, I fancy,' he observed with satisfaction. 'As Louis would say, there's confusion amongst them. Recharge all the muskets,' he added, as he set about reloading the gun that had done so much damage.

Algy grinned as he looked at him, for his face was black with powder smoke. 'As you say, that should have given them something to think about,' he agreed. 'Do you think they'll try it again?'

'There's no knowing what they'll try,' growled Biggles. 'Deutch is desperate for the doubloons, and he'll try everything before he gives up. If all else fails, he may try to starve us out, in which case, since we've no means of leaving the island, things may get awkward.'

'Talking about starving, what about cracking the odd nut?' suggested Dick. 'I'm hungry.'

A bullet splashed against the parapet.

'You'll get your own nut cracked if you don't keep it down,' Biggles told him grimly. 'I saw you dancing about while the fight was on as if there were no such things as bullets.'

Dick raised his eyebrows. 'Did they shoot at us?'

'I should jolly well think they did. The rest of the crowd, hidden amongst the rocks opposite, were sniping at us as fast as they could go. Don't forget that next time. All right; go below everybody and get a bite. I'll keep watch. Come up and take over when you've finished eating.'

The afternoon wore on, and by the time the others had finished, and Biggles had snatched a hasty meal, the sun was far down in the west. There was no sign of the enemy apart from an occasional shot that smacked harmlessly against the parapet, which served as a warning that the islet was being closely watched.

In the twilight four men made a dash towards the boat,

but they had no heart for their job and beat a quick retreat under the fusillade poured at them from the ramparts. Twilight deepened into night, but there was no further activity on the island.

'We shall have to keep strict watch tonight,' declared Biggles. 'We had better make our beds up here. Dick, no prowling about, remember.'

Dick shook his head vigorously. 'Don't you worry about that,' he said with an emphasis that made them all laugh.

Chapter 16

Warm Work

Dawn the following morning saw Algy doing duty as guard. A slight mist hung over the sea and shrouded the island in a soft, lavender-tinted mantle, but as the rays of the sun dispersed it, his sharply uttered, 'All hands to repel boarders' brought the others scrambling to their feet.

'What's happening?' demanded Biggles tersely, wide awake on the instant.

Algy pointed, and following the direction of his outstretched finger, the others saw the coaster, which was really a ketch fitted with an auxiliary engine, standing towards them over a flat sea that shimmered with all the hues of mother-of-pearl. With the island background, the tall mainmast reflected faithfully in the water, and the long ripple of the wake flashing like a jewelled chain, the boat made a delightful picture. 'A painted ship upon a painted ocean.' But Biggles saw no beauty in the scene, for her mission was all too clear.

'So that's the idea,' he murmured quietly. 'They're going to try to board us from the big boat. Unless I'm mistaken, this is where things start to warm up.'

'I can't see anybody, except the man at the wheel,' remarked Algy, one foot on the low parapet, leaning against his cutlass as he regarded the oncoming ship with brooding eyes.

'Don't be deceived by that. I imagine they are all below, out of reach of our shot – or so they think. They know all about the swivel-gun now, but they know nothing about

173

our heavy metal. If only we can aim straight we can still give them a jolt. Listen, chaps,' he went on earnestly. 'We've talked a lot about Louis le Grande, and we've played at being pirates, but there is going to be no fun about this. We're facing reality, even if the clock has been put back two hundred and fifty years. We've got to fight because we can do nothing else. It would be fatal to fall into Deutch's hands. We know too much, and he'd see to it that we didn't pop up at some future date to lay evidence against him for murder. "Dead men tell no tales" is his motto. It was Dakeyne's, under whose flag we are fighting, so we may as well make it ours. If Deutch wins, it will be a case of "Them as die'll be the lucky ones", as Long John Silver would say, so we'll fight as men were expected to fight in the days when the Jolly Roger flapped at the peak. That's all.' Stooping, he snapped his pistol in the little heap of powder he had prepared, and after the flash, stirred the rags it had ignited. 'Come on,' he added. 'Let's have the guns over to this side and stand by to give them a broadside.'

Dick helped to drag the heavy guns into position, and again the feeling came over him that he was living in the past; that he was doing something he had done before in some other age. But there was no time for contemplation.

'The skunks are taking good care to keep out of sight,' muttered Biggles, as he watched the approaching boat.

'What is the maximum range of these guns, do you think?' asked Algy.

'I haven't the foggiest notion,' confessed Biggles. 'I've handled a good many different weapons in my life, but not this sort. They were a bit before my time. All the same, I've taken a great fancy to them.'

'Try a sighting shot; we should be able to reach them now,' suggested Algy.

'Yes, I think we may as well open the ball,' agreed Biggles. 'Stand clear when I fire; she'll jump like a wild horse. Get ready to reload.' He crouched behind the gun, squinting through the small round hole that served as a crude sight. 'Get a light, Algy,' he ordered, as he made a slight adjustment in alignment.

Algy snatched up a piece of glowing rag on the end of his cutlass and stood ready.

'Fire!' shouted Biggles, jumping aside.

A long tongue of orange flame, followed instantly by a churning cloud of smoke, leapt out across the sea as the gun exploded like a thunderclap and jerked backwards under the power of the recoil. While the echoes were still reverberating in the hills a column of water spurted into the air beyond the boat, now about a quarter of a mile away.

'You're over her,' cried Algy, stooping down to peer under the smoke. 'Your line was good; a little less elevation and you'll hit her.'

'I'll get the hang of it in a minute,' answered Biggles, darting to the next gun, while Dick and Ginger started reloading the one he had just fired. Algy stood ready with the rag.

'Fire!'

Boom!

Again a stream of flame and smoke flashed towards the boat. There was a crash of timber and a cloud of splinters flew from her counter.

'Got her!' yelled Algy delightedly. 'Keep it up.'

'We've got to land one in her engine-room, or hole her at the water-line,' muttered Biggles. 'In the old days they could shoot at the rigging to put a ship out of action, but that doesn't work any longer – more's the pity. Now we've got the range we'll give her a broadside; it should put the wind up them, at any rate.'

Again Ginger and Dick reloaded feverishly while Biggles sighted the other guns.

'Everyone get some rag and stand by to fire,' he cried. 'Ready! *Fire!*'

The fort shook under the roar of the guns. A huge cloud of smoke completely hid the target. While it was clearing they all worked like madmen at reloading.

'Hurrah!' Algy's cheer was taken up by the others as the smoke cleared sufficiently for them to see the ship.

'You've got her mast,' shouted Dick, dancing in his excitement.

It was true. The mainmast trailed over the starboard quarter. This, of course, did not affect the boat as it would have done had it been under sail, but the extra resistance on one side caused her to yaw.* The crew had evidently realized it and were trying to correct the trouble, for three men were slashing furiously at the tangled cordage to clear it. Half the wooden superstructure had also been carried away, so it was clear that at least two shots had found their mark.

'Muskets!' roared Biggles. 'Try to drop those fellows who are clearing the tackle. If we can stop them it may foul the rudder.'

They opened up a brisk fire with their small-arms. One of the men dropped; another bolted. The third, with commendable courage – for the range was short – braved the fire and went on with his work.

Biggles dropped his musket, sprang to the swivel-gun, took quick aim, and fired. His aim was true. The deadly grape-shot swept the deck and sent splinters flying in all directions. The one survivor of the working party dropped, but after rolling about for a moment or two, he managed to get to his hands and knees and crawl away to cover.

Biggles was astonished at the effect caused by the gun,

---

* Turn unsteadily from side to side.

and he expressed it. 'It's more effective than shrapnel,' he declared. 'We stung her badly that time – look.'

The boat was now definitely veering off its course, although the helmsman, whom they could see crouching in the damaged superstructure, had got his rudder hard over.

'Ginger, Algy, go on firing the big stuff,' shouted Biggles. 'Don't wait for me. Load and fire as fast as you can. Dick, re-load all the muskets.'

They began a furious cannonade, Biggles using the swivel-gun, the others firing solid ball. The boat was hit several times; her planking was torn and furrowed; splinters lay everywhere, both about the decks and on the water, but in spite of their efforts, the helmsman managed to get his craft under control and it crept steadily nearer.

Biggles began to look anxious, for he saw that within a few minutes she would pass inside the field of fire of their guns, the muzzles of which were already depressed almost to their limits. Further, she had gone out to pass the islet on the seaward side, presumably to reach the steps, which Deutch had either seen or assumed were there, and time was lost while they dragged the guns to point in that direction.

On the other hand, the range was now point-blank, and a shot, when one went home, did a tremendous amount of damage, although, as the soldiers were still below deck, it was impossible to estimate the actual execution. Between the roar of the guns and the crash of striking shot, the gunners on the rocks could hear Deutch's furious cursing as he drove the crew on. Above the islet a mighty cloud of white smoke was mushrooming slowly into the air.

Biggles, perspiration streaming down through the grime on his face, tore off his shirt and flung it aside. 'Keep your heads down,' he shouted, as bullets began to whistle through the air or smack against the parapet. He dragged the swivel-gun into a fresh position and poured a withering hail of lead almost vertically into the coaster's deck. It was his last shot, for with that she crept within the zone of fire and began edging towards the landing steps. He saw that if she reached them the position would become desperate, but it was hard to see how it could be prevented. They had battered the ship to pieces, but her engines were still running; as he had said earlier on, had she been a sailing vessel she would have been out of action long before.

Algy snatched up a musket, took deliberate aim at the helmsman, and fired. A splinter of wood flew into the air near the fellow's head, causing him to duck, but did no further damage. Algy tossed the discharged weapon to Dick, who was panting with heat and excitement, and grabbed another. He fired again, and grunted his satisfaction as the man fell, howling, clutching at an arm that dangled uselessly.

'Hold your fire, everybody,' roared Biggles. 'Wait till they show themselves, then let them have it. Look out! Stand clear!'

He had seen that the vessel was now alongside the landing-stage, which was immediately under where they stood, crushing their canoe flat. While the others were still wondering what he was going to do, he had dragged one of the big guns round until the muzzle was pointing at the inside of the rampart wall, and flung a glowing rag across the touch-hole. The hot blast of the explosion made them stagger, gasping in the swirling smoke through which they saw that a large part of the wall had disappeared. The mass of masonry crashed down on the vessel's deck. Shouts and groans filled the air; bullets smacked viciously, or screamed as they richochetted off the rock.

Dick, fighting mad for the first time in his life, began

heaving cannon-balls through the breach in the wall, cheering hoarsely as he did so.

It gave Biggles an idea. 'Hi! Algy!' he yelled, straining at the gun he had just fired.

Algy saw what he was trying to do, and joined him. The others rushed to their assistance. Between them they trundled the gun to the edge of the fort. 'Right over!' roared Biggles.

For a moment the mass of iron hung poised on the brink; then it toppled over. With a frightful crash it landed on the deck of the vessel below; it went straight through the top deck as if the planking had been tissue paper, and disappeared from sight. The boat shuddered under the weight of the impact.

Deutch, with half a dozen men at his heels, appeared, making for the steps.

'Muskets!' yelled Biggles, snatching up the nearest. He took careful aim at Deutch and pulled the trigger. The hammer fell with a splutter of sparks as the weapon misfired. Deutch, by this time halfway up the steps, his teeth showing in an ugly snarl, threw up his automatic. Biggles hurled the musket at him. It struck him on the arm, knocking the weapon out of his hand. Deutch, without pausing in his rush, whipped out a knife. Biggles snatched up a pistol and fired; the shot missed Deutch but knocked over the man behind him. Pandemonium reigned. Biggles, looking frantically for another pistol, flinched as a weapon exploded in his ears, temporarily deafening him. He saw that Algy had fired it. Another of the attackers flung up his arms and went backwards, carrying one of his comrades off the steps with him as he fell. Deutch, mouthing like a maniac, came on and reached the top; two others were close behind.

Biggles, weaponless, looked round for one, and saw a cutlass lying where it had got knocked over in the fray. He turned to get it, but his foot caught in the broken masonry of the wall, and he fell headlong. Deutch leapt at him like a wild cat. His arm jerked up, the knife flashing in the sun. Biggles wriggled like an eel to avoid the blow, but the sailor's legs were over his own, pinning them down. For a split second they remained thus, and then, at the precise moment that the knife began to descend, a pistol roared. Deutch stiffened, arm still upraised; it dropped to his side and he fell over, coughing.

Biggles flung him off and sprang to his feet. Dick, white as death, was crouching a yard away, a smoking pistol in his hand.

'Good work, Dick,' gasped Biggles, breathlessly, for it had been a narrow escape. He snatched up the cutlass. But during the second that he had been on the ground the whole position had changed. The sole survivor of the boarders, seeing Deutch fall and finding himself alone, waited for no more. He saw Biggles and Algy bearing down on him from either side, cutlasses in their hands. Flinging aside his rifle, he jumped clear off the rock into the sea. The few men left on the deck of the boat were working furiously to push it off.

'All right! Cease fire!' ordered Biggles, and looked about him.

Algy was leaning against the wall, his hat gone, his hair on end, perspiration streaming down his face as he reloaded his pistol. Dick was staring down at the ship, wild-eyed. Ginger, pale under a thick layer of black powder-dust, was sitting down, mopping blood off his cheek with a piece of his shirt.

'Are you hurt?' cried Biggles sharply.

'Nothing to write home about,' answered Ginger weakly. 'A bullet knocked off a piece of rock and it hit me in the face.'

Biggles looked back at the ship, now fifty yards away,

and making straight for the shore. 'They've had enough,' he said. 'By the shades of Morgan, Louis himself never saw a brisker five minutes than that.' He struck the top off a coconut with his cutlass and handed it to Ginger. 'Take a sip,' he invited.

'What I need is a bucket of water,' growled Ginger, as he staggered to his feet. 'I've never been so hot in my life. Where's the boat?'

'If you mean ours, it's sunk,' replied Biggles. 'It was crushed flat. If you mean theirs, they seem to be running it ashore. Those who are left have evidently had enough for one day. So have I, if it comes to that. Keep your heads down; some skunk might decide to take a last crack at us. Did anyone see Harvey in the fight? I was looking for him because he's the only one who can get away in our machine.'

'No, I didn't see him,' answered Algy.

'Nor I,' echoed the others.

'That's a nuisance. I'm afraid he'll make off in the machine before we can get to it,' muttered Biggles, with a worried frown. He walked to the opposite side of the fort and looked towards the lagoon. A movement on his left caught his eye, and he turned sharply seaward, staring incredulously. 'What the dickens is this?' he cried.

The others, sensing more danger, ran to his side. Less than a mile away, racing towards the island, her bows throwing up two tall feathers of spray, was a dark, slim, rakish-looking craft.

'Great Scott, it's a destroyer!' muttered Dick. 'If she's after us, we've got our work cut out, and no mistake.'

'She isn't. She's British,' cried Biggles excitedly. I can see her ensign.' He looked at the others. 'Trust the Navy to pop up when anything's going on,' he murmured. 'I don't know what they'll say when they see this mess; buccaneering is a bit out of date. Well, we can only wait and see. Frankly, I'm not sorry to see her; a coconut diet may sound fine in books, but personally I'm pining to look a plate of ham and eggs in the face again.'

Leaning against the wall, they could see the destroyer's rail lined with inquisitive spectators, all looking in their direction.

'What about giving them three cheers?' suggested Ginger. 'That should let them know we're British, anyway.'

'Good idea,' agreed Biggles. 'Let 'em rip. Hip-hip—'

Raising their voices, they sent three rousing cheers floating over the water; but there was no answering cheer from the destroyer.

'Miserable blighters,' grumbled Algy.

'You've heard talk of the Silent Service; now you can see it,' grinned Biggles.

The destroyer's bow-wave dropped away suddenly as she slowed down. Before she had run to a standstill a boat was on the water, six pairs of oars flashing as it sped towards them. A dapper lieutenant in white ducks sat in the stern.

'Round the other side,' shouted Biggles, as he saw him looking for a landing-place.

A crisp word of command and the boat altered its course; it rounded the islet, and a moment later came to rest at the landing-stage. The officer stepped ashore, staring about him in astonishment at the signs of the conflict. The sailors in the boat grinned up at the four faces peering down at them.

The officer ran lightly up the steps and then stood still, an expression of comical astonishment on his face as his eyes ran over the guns and the four grotesque, powder-grimed figures. 'Just what do you think you're playing at?' he asked curtly.

Biggles frowned. 'Playing?' he queried. 'This sort of thing may be all fun and games to you, but I can assure you that

182

during the last hour some very strenuous work has been put in on this blistering rock. If you don't believe that, you try sticking cannon-balls down a muzzle-loader on a hot day.'

The other smiled faintly. The black flag caught his eye. 'Pirates, eh?' he murmured.

'Something of the sort,' agreed Biggles, carelessly.

'Sort of Treasure Island?'

'Precisely!' declared Biggles. 'Allow me to introduce myself. Captain Smollett, at your service. The gentleman on my left is Squire Trelawny; on my right – with the busted cheek – is Doctor Live-say and young Jim Hawkins.' He pointed to the huddled body of Deutch. 'And there's Long John Silver,' he added.

The other started. 'Is he dead?'

'I hope so,' answered Biggles frankly. 'He deserves to be, anyway. If he is it will save the hangman a job.'

The officer shook his head as if the affair was beyond him – as indeed it was. His manner suggested that he thought he was dealing with madmen. Did you get the treasure?' he inquired politely.

Biggles raised his eyebrows. 'Of course; otherwise the story would be all wrong, wouldn't it? There it is; help yourself to a doubloon or two for luck.'

The officer stepped forward, and Biggles, watching him, saw that he was about to pick up a doubloon that lay just under Deutch's pocket. He jumped forward and snatched it up. 'Not that one,' he said grimly. 'Touch that, and you'll never make another landfall. There is only one place for that particular piece.' With a quick jerk of his arm he sent Bawn's doubloon skimming through the air. For a brief moment the sunlight flashed on it as it dropped through space; then, with a tiny splash, it disappeared into the sea. Biggles breathed a sigh of relief as he turned back to the lieutenant. 'There's a story hanging to it,' he explained quietly.

The other nodded. 'I think you'd better come and tell it to Captain Crocker,' he said.

'That's a good idea,' agreed Biggles.

In single file they followed the officer down the steps into the boat.

Chapter 17

Explanations

'It was a bit of luck for us that you happened to be coming this way,' observed Biggles, as they sped towards the destroyer.

The officer smiled. 'Luck, do you call it?' he said. 'Do you think everyone is deaf? You made enough row to be heard over half the West Indies. We could see the smoke twenty miles away, and as we don't like wars starting on British islands – at least, not without knowing what they're about – we came along to see.'

Biggles laughed, and glanced at the destroyer's rail, lined with curious, expectant faces. He turned to speak to the others, but the expression on Dick's face caused the words to remain unsaid. His eyes were round, and his face was as white as a sheet under its grime. Suddenly he buried his face in his hands.

'Here, what's the matter, laddie?' cried Biggles sharply, thinking perhaps he had received a wound which he had tried to conceal.

Dick shook his head. 'It's nothing,' he said.

Come on, out with it,' insisted Biggles.

I thought – I saw – my father; up there on deck,' whispered Dick.

Biggles looked sharply at the little crowd lining the rails. A civilian, an elderly man with grey hair, was conspicuous.

'Who's that?' he asked the officer tensely.

But the lieutenant was looking at Dick. 'Your name isn't Denver by any chance, is it?' he asked quickly.

.'Yes – Dick Denver,' answered Dick wonderingly.

'Well, that's about the last straw,' muttered the officer unbelievingly. 'We've got your father aboard. He went to the Admiral at Kingston with a wild tale about a treasure and a galleon, and the Admiral was so interested that he sent him out with us to locate the island. How in thunder did you get here?'

But Dick barely heard him. As the boat touched the steps that had been lowered, without waiting for permission he jumped on to them and raced to the top.

By the time the others reached the deck he was laughing and crying at once in the elderly man's arms, while a circle of officers and ratings looked on wonderingly.

'This certainly beats all the stories I've ever read into a cocked hat,' whispered Biggles to Algy, as the officer who had escorted them invited them to follow him to an awning on the after deck, where the commander was waiting.

Captain Crocker was a young man. With his officers behind him, he regarded the curiously garbed, battle-stained quartet with interest, suspicion, and some slight amusement. 'Sit down,' he said. 'I should like to know what's going on here. Who is in charge of this – er – party?'

Biggles stepped forward. 'I am,' he answered; 'but before I satisfy your very natural curiosity, may I make three suggestions, all of which have a considerable degree of urgency, or I would not make them now. First of all, a bucket or two of cold water for internal and external use; secondly, that you send a party to take charge of my aircraft, which you can see over there in the lagoon; and lastly, that you send a shore party to the rock we have just evacuated in order to take possession of a fairly valuable collection of gold coins which, as you will no doubt rightly assume, was the primary cause of the undignified bickering that was in progress at the moment of your opportune arrival. You see,' he explained, 'a few of the enemy have survived the engagement, and while I do not think it is probable, there is just a chance that they may make a final raid. If, at the same time, while your men are on the spot, they could dispose of some of the casualties which at present litter an otherwise pleasant spot, so much the better.'

The commander stared at Biggles. 'Do you mean to say that you've actually found a treasure?'

'There are about fifty thousand doubloons kicking about loose on that rock,' murmured Biggles evenly.

'Good heavens!'

'There you are, sir, I told you they were not far away,' cried Dick's father, who was present.

'As a matter of detail, sir, there are a lot of interesting things on this island,' observed Biggles quietly.

'Have you found the galleon that we've heard about?'

'Yes, I'll show you over it presently, if you like; but at the moment we are badly in need of some refreshment.'

The commander got up. 'Quite – quite,' he said. 'I'm still all at sea – but have a wash and a drink; then you can tell me about it. Meanwhile, I'll send parties to do as you suggest.'

'Thanks,' nodded Biggles.

While they were washing, Dick exchanged rapid explanations with his father who, it appeared, had survived the knife wound, but only after a long, painful illness. As soon as he was convalescent he had written a second letter to Dick, but by that time Dick was already on his way to the island, so he did not receive it. As soon as he – Dick's father – was well enough to travel he had worked a passage to Kingston, Jamaica, and there told his highly improbable story to the Admiral commanding the West Indian Station. The Admiral was sceptical about the treasure, but the story of the galleon, still intact, had aroused his curiosity, and he had dispatched a destroyer to investigate, with Dick's father to point out the island, and, when it was found, show the captain where the wreck lay hidden.

These things had only occurred during the last few days. On the previous evening they had picked up a wireless message, sent out by the Pan-American radio station at Marabina, to the effect that four British airmen were missing in the locality and it was for the aeroplane that the destroyer was really searching when the sound of heavy gun-fire was heard. Not a little astonished, she had steamed at full speed in the direction of the supposed battle, with the result that is now known. Dick's father was, of course, just as astonished to see Dick as Dick was to see him.

An hour later, after a square meal, they again forgathered under the awning. The Sikorsky had been towed to the destroyer, and now floated lightly close at hand on the limpid water. The doubloons lay in a pile near the commander's chair. Presently he joined them. 'There seem to have been some nice goings-on here,' he said seriously. 'Take your time and let me have the whole story.'

Whereupon, seated in a deck-chair with a drink at his elbow, Biggles told the tale of their adventures from beginning to end to a spellbound audience. The manner in which they had held the islet particularly intrigued the naval officers.

'It sounds more like a book than a true story,' observed the commander when Biggles had finished. 'By the way, this treasure will have to be regarded as Treasure Trove – that is, Crown property – anyway, until there has been a Court of Inquiry.'

'I know; I made provision for that before I left England,' replied Biggles. 'As a matter of fact, I have a document, issued by the Treasury with the concurrence of the Admiralty, stating that we are to take fifty per cent of anything we find, after deducting expenses. I think we shall be quite happy with our share.'

'I should think you ought to be, too,' smiled the commander. 'By the way, amongst the dead on the boat there is a fellow who looks like an Englishman. According to the papers in his pocket, his name was Harvey—'

'Ah! That's the chap who stole our machine at Marabina,' put in Biggles quickly. 'I wondered what happened to him. I imagine he went into partnership with Deutch.'

'Well, I'm taking some of my officers ashore. We are all anxious to see the old ship, and the fort on the rock. Naturally, we are professionally interested. Would you like to come and show us round?'

'With pleasure,' agreed Biggles. 'In fact, we'd like to have another look round ourselves.'

They spent the rest of the day ashore, exploring thoroughly the old fort and the interior of the once-stately galleon, with which the naval officers were entranced, declaring it to be of great historical importance. A guard was set over it, and only when it was too dark to see more did the party return to the destroyer, Dick taking with him Dakeyne's black flag, which he got permission to retain.

They spent the night on board the destroyer, but with the rising of the sun preparations were made for departure, Captain Crocker, who had reported the discovery by radio to his Admiral, having received a signal instructing him to proceed at once to headquarters. He offered to give the airmen a lift, but they declined, preferring to travel their own way. They arranged to meet at Kingston, however, where it was thought that the official inquiry would be held.

As the destroyer's anchor emerged from the blue water Biggles started the Sikorsky's engines. Aircraft and water-craft moved forward together, the destroyer slowly, the amphibian with ever increasing speed. The destroyer dipped her ensign as the aircraft forged ahead, but the salute of her siren was lost in the roar of the Sikorsky's motors as she soared into the air.

Ten minutes later, when Dick looked behind, Treasure Island was a blue line on the horizon.

There is little more to tell. After the Admiralty Court, held in the West Indies, where the discovery of the galleon and the treasure was a nine days' wonder, Dick, his father, and the three airmen took passage for London, where the final claims for the treasure had been lodged. It realized rather more than two hundred thousand pounds, of which one-half was held to be the property of the Crown. The remainder was divided between the adventurers in the proportions agreed upon.

Dick was in two minds whether to follow the sea or the air as a career; in the end, to please his father and follow the traditions of his family, he was entered as an apprentice in the Merchant Service. Today, in the cabin of 'Doubloon Dick', as he is called – for his story is well known – hangs a trophy that is the envy of every other apprentice in his ship. It is a black flag; the sinister banner of Louis Dakeyne, Louis le Grande, The Exterminator.